PRAISE FOR MARNI MANN

UNBLOCKED, EPISODE ONE

"This was a fantastic opener to a series, and it was much steamier than I was expecting. Told in both POV's, the chemistry between Frankie & Derek was sizzling. The characters were both likeable and I am dying for the next one to see their relationship develop."

—Arabella, I Love Book Love Blog

"Her writing style was flawless, her descriptions felt so decadent, she held me hostage with her words from the minute I started this book and left me craving for more. This story was a scorching premise of a series that promises nothing short of a passionate and thrilling ride…"

—Dee Montoya, Goodreads Reviewer

"Wow. This was a scorching read. Ms. Mann created a swirl of sexual tension that knocked you off balance. I instantly felt drawn into this story, which is a must when it comes to creating a serial series."

—Michelle New, Goodreads Reviewer

UNBLOCKED, EPISODE TWO

"Unblocked is, without a doubt the current serial every erotic reader should be seeking out and devouring. If you haven't already started I highly recommend you jump in and experience Derek and Frankie. Bask in the excitement and anticipation as each episode is revealed."

—Jxxx PinkLady, Goodreads Reviewer

"This episode is Super Super Sexy. Marni Mann writes sex scenes that are explosive and passionate. The chemistry between Derek and Frankie is palpable and erotic. He is a man that knows what he wants and goes after it with fierce determination. But once he has Frankie, will once be enough?"

—Deanna PinkLady, Goodreads Reviewer

"Episode two has my complete undivided attention NOW!!! The sexual chemistry of Derek Block and Frankie Jordan was an inferno!! The sex, passion, dirty talks, and seduction…was off the charts!!! Marni Mann has turned up the notch and heat level in this installment. If you wanted a book to devour and re-read again, hands down it would be episode two."

—Michelle Tan, Four Chicks Flipping Pages

UNBLOCKED:
EPISODE 3

MARNI MANN

ISBN-13 978-1533084026

To Susan and Irwin, a
perfect picture of love.
Thanks for being an
inspiration and for
allowing me to capture it.

ONE.

DEREK

I was waiting for my cup of coffee to brew when I heard the front door of my townhouse open, and heels clicking on the wood floor. Hayden had left just a minute ago, but must have forgotten something; there was no other reason she'd be back so soon. Frankie wasn't due for another ten minutes, and she wouldn't have come in without knocking…especially not after telling me she never wanted me to touch her again.

Never again.

I gripped the mug with both hands, my teeth grinding

together as the swishing of fabric and clicking of heels got louder.

"I need coffee," my sister said as she entered my kitchen. She moved with much more steam than when she'd left.

I handed her the full mug and brewed another. "Check the fridge," I said. "I think there's some of that vanilla creamer you like in there."

"I won't ask why you have it." She poured in a few drops and placed it back in the door. "I'm not here enough for you to stock it, and you drink your coffee black." She walked to the island, her eyes widening as she looked at the granite. "Is it safe to lean on this counter, or did you have her on the surface of this, too?"

"Have who?"

"The girl who takes vanilla creamer in her coffee."

Hayden looked rough this morning, which had a lot to do with the bottle of Jack we had polished off last night, and the four hours of sleep that had followed. "I know you didn't come back for coffee. What's on your mind?"

She shrugged and looked around the kitchen, her hands fidgeting with the cup. "You're usually at Timber Towers well before eight. It's almost nine now so why are you still here?"

"I needed a little sleep."

"Bullshit. You function fine without sleep."

"Well, I'm hung over, too."

"I'm calling bullshit again. You never get anything more than a headache, which a few aspirin can take care of." She sat up straighter and held the mug under her chin. "Maybe you're expecting someone?" I could read Hayden better than anyone. Her bark was coarse and unforgiving, almost always misinterpreted—characteristics that made her a very successful lawyer. That was how I knew her shaking hands weren't just from a hangover. Something had gotten to her...or someone.

"My real estate agent is coming over," I told her.

"Your agent?"

I walked to her side of the island and put my arm around her shoulders. "The one I hired for Timber Towers."

"And what's this real estate agent's name?"

I smelled whiskey and hairspray that blended with her coffee. She was right: all I'd woken up to this morning was a headache, and now the scents in the room were making it worse. "I hope you don't have an important meeting in the next hour or so, because it doesn't look like you're going to make it."

She took a side step and turned to face me, gripping her cup like I might try to steal it. "No meeting, but I have to get home to shower...*I* do have to go into work today." She finally took her eyes off the mug and looked at me. "What's your agent's name, Derek?" she asked again.

"Her name is Frankie Jordan." An emotion passed over her face. It happened quickly, and left as fast as it came. "Hayden, is everything okay?" The only time I'd ever seen that look was when she spoke about the bastards from her past.

"I've got to get going. Walk me to the door?"

I slid my arm around her shoulders again, holding her tightly as we moved to the foyer. It didn't feel like she needed me to keep her steady physically, but I felt like she needed the support somehow. I wondered what had shaken her in the short time she had left my place and came back...and why she wouldn't answer me.

"Stay here," I said, opening the front door, "I'll catch you a cab."

"No, I'm good. I'm going to walk for a bit."

She hated mornings. She hated the cold even more and this was a bitter one. Something was definitely eating at her. "You sure about that?" She went down the front steps without responding and turned when she reached the sidewalk, holding out her mug. "Keep it," I said. "I'll get it later."

"Right." Her eyes followed several cars that drove by before she faced me. "Frankie might have stopped by earlier when I was on my way out."

"She *might* have?"

She nodded.

"And you recognized her?"

"I know who she is...she seemed to be in a rush to leave." She took a sip. "Looks like your meeting got canceled, brother. Thought you should know." She waved as she dragged herself down the sidewalk.

It didn't surprise me that she had heard of Frankie; she had done enough digging on Randy to know anyone of importance in the real estate industry. What surprised me was that Frankie had come here, and had left without making contact.

I pulled out my phone and hit Frankie's name in my contacts, and hung up when I got her voicemail. Where the fuck was she? And what was so goddamn important that she had taken off without telling me? I hung up when I got her voicemail a second time and went back into the kitchen.

Bailing on a meeting wasn't like her. She was the type to keep her promises, and she had promised to be here…and I had promised not to touch her. That was going to be difficult.

Maybe she'd just gone to grab some coffee…

I went into the office that was off the kitchen and booted up my computer, scanning the emails that filled my inbox. None were from her. Neither was the text message that appeared onto my phone…or the one that followed. I took my time replying to both and to the emails that required a prompt response.

When I looked at the clock again, it was almost nine-thirty.

I wasn't just the man who knew the intimate angles of her pussy; I was her client, goddammit. Just like she wanted me to be.

Fuck this.

I opened our last text message conversation and started typing:

You'd better have a hell of a good reason for not being here right now.

She usually responded immediately, but the bubble under her name that showed she was typing didn't appear. When several minutes passed with no reply, I called Will. "Have you heard from Frankie's office?"

"Not a thing," he said. "Why?"

"Hayden said Frankie pulled up to my townhouse this

morning, then took off without coming inside. She still hasn't returned."

"Maybe she doesn't trust herself at your place?"

Will knew so much—not just about my business; my personal life, too. "Nah. She has more self-control than that. Backing out isn't her style. She finishes what she starts."

"Hold on for a second."

He put me on hold, and I finished my coffee and stuck the cup in the dishwasher. The sound of a vacuum came from the second floor; my housekeeper was working on the bedrooms now that Hayden and I were out of them. Since my dick had become fixated on Frankie's cunt, the stream of women passing through my bedroom had disappeared, and she had a lot less to clean. There was a notable absence of used condoms in the trash, washcloths in the bathroom, tissues and panties on the floor. The woman deserved a small fortune for picking up after me. And if I couldn't persuade my gorgeous pink ivory to let me taste her again, things would soon go back to the way they had been.

It wasn't time to consider that yet.

Will clicked over. "Brea hasn't seen her either," he said. "She thought Frankie was with you."

Brea wouldn't rat out her boss. She knew exactly where Frankie was, and it wasn't with me.

"I'll see you in twenty," I said, and we both hung up.

TWO.

FRANKIE

A text message from Brea lit up my screen, telling me that Will had called the office and inquired on my whereabouts. I hadn't returned Derek's phone calls or text when they came; I fully expected my office to be the next in line. I knew I should have replied, should have used some excuse about an emergency having arisen. But every time I attempted to write back, the image of that woman walking out of his townhouse would shoot through my mind, and my entire body started to shake. It had been hard enough making the decision to keep things between us platonic. Seeing how he had moved on so quickly—and with her, of all people—was just too much.

Instead of replying to Brea's text, I called. "We're going out tonight," I said as she answered. "Can you leave the office before five?"

"No problem, boss lady."

I'd spent the last few hours holed up in my condo. There was probably chocolate in my hair and on my shirt, and I was positive it was under my nails. I needed a long soak in the tub and a pedicure…maybe even some touch-up waxing. "I'll call you when I'm on my way," I said.

I hung up, tossed the throw off my legs and stood from the couch, headed for the bathroom. Derek had once told me I wasn't allowed to masturbate unless he gave me permission. He'd controlled my orgasms, even from a distance. But he didn't control anything anymore, and I intended on proving that the minute I got into the tub, when I buried two fingers deep inside me and let the water from the jets caress my clit.

"I'm almost positive we don't have to cheers after the third glass of wine," I said. Still, I hit my glass against Brea's. I was more than a little buzzed and could no longer feel my wrist—or my fingers, or my lips…

"No way…we need to, girl." She paused to hiccup. "I feel like it's been so long since we've gotten wasted together—and *damn*, it feels so good."

She was right about that. The last time we'd had a drink together was the afternoon we had run into Derek and Julia having lunch, before the contract, before the sex. So much had changed in such a short time.

"It's been ten days since we've had wine," I practically

shouted. It was past happy hour and the dinner crowd was filling the bar, making it difficult to hear.

"That's still too long. Pre-D, we used to get drinks at least twice a week."

"Pre-D?"

She nodded, her eyes widening and her lips spreading into a silly grin. "D for Derek. Or Derek's capital-D Dick. Whichever you prefer. Both are large and gorgeous and beyond perfect."

"Oh God…I tell you way too much." I lifted my wine and took a huge sip. "Well, it's now post-D, so we'll be having many more happy hours like this."

She leaned into the narrow high-top to get closer, her arms crossing over the table. "The wine wants me to tell you something."

My brows rose. "What would that be?"

"You're the one who decided to end things. You can't be upset with him for moving on. It's not like he knew you had a past with that chick."

I remembered the text message I had seen on his phone from Hayden the morning after we had spent the night together. *I need to see you tonight.*

"But he barely even waited a day, Brea. That's just wrong."

The candle on the table made her teeth glow and showed how big her smile was—I knew that grin, and I knew what it meant. "You wanted him to fight for you, didn't you?"

When I told him I wanted to end things physically, he acted as though he agreed. He didn't resist; he didn't argue. He just complied. Then minutes later, his text asked me to come to his townhouse the next morning. Was that his way of fighting for me, or was he trying to make sure our professional relationship stayed smooth? I didn't know. All I *did* know was seeing that woman come out of his place made my entire body ache. I hated that his dominant hands and ravenous lips had been all over her—*her* or any woman, really. I didn't want to share him…but he wasn't mine, and now he never would be. "Let's order a shot." I raised my hand to call over our waitress. "What do you want? Tequila? Bourbon?"

"Slow down there, little lady," Brea slurred. "Shots and wine aren't a good combination. Don't you remember that from the morning after the gala?"

"Two shots of tequila, please," I said to the waitress. I glanced at Brea's scowl. "And two extra-large waters."

Brea put her hand on top of mine. "It's okay to like him. It's okay to feel something for him. And it's okay to talk about it."

I shook my head, the wine making my brain tingle. "He's not someone I'm supposed to have feelings for. He's not..." My thoughts drifted to our night at the hotel, how it had felt when his attention was focused on me, how my body had responded to it. No man had ever gotten me to bend, to buck, to scream the way Derek had. Our connection was more than just physical; I knew that the moment he had touched me. It wouldn't have been that intense if there weren't some level of emotional involvement. "He's not what I need right now. He could never settle down...I think he proved that pretty clearly this morning. And I can't handle another Reed situation." I took a breath. "I just can't."

"Oh shit." The look on her face concerned me. "Whatever you do, do not turn around. We've been spotted."

"By who?"

She didn't get a chance to respond. A second later, Reed appeared at our table. "Brea," he said, nodding. His eyes slowly moved to me, and his hand cupped my shoulder. I started to shake it off just as he moved it away. "Frankie, I didn't know you were still coming here." His eyes narrowed.

When Reed and I were together, we came to this bar frequently; it was close to both our offices, which made it an easy meeting place. It was also a favorite of Brea's, and only a few blocks from her apartment, which was the reason we were here now. I hadn't even thought about whether Reed would be here too.

"I don't usually," I replied.

He gripped the stem of my glass, giving the wine a quick swirl, looking over the top of it. "A 2012 reserve? Let me buy you another—"

"No," Brea and I said at the same time.

"Thank you," I continued, "but we've had plenty."

"We definitely have," Brea confirmed.

"Fair enough." He released the glass and moved closer, his hand returning to my shoulder.

Everything about his touch felt wrong...and his scent, and his pleading eyes, and the way his cufflinks rubbed against my skin. I wanted to feel soft flannel and a strong grip, to be filled with the scent of spice and woods, to feel the heat from an electric blue gaze. I wanted dominance in its rawest form, not refinement.

I wanted Derek.

I wanted him more than I was willing to admit out loud, although the wine was making it much easier.

"Brea," Reed said, "I'm going to steal her for just a minute."

"No, he's not—"

He cut me off. "Walk with me, Frankie." His lips were practically pressing against my ear. I felt nothing; no warmth, no tingling between my legs. "I won't keep you long."

"Two minutes, Reed. Not a second more." I pulled myself out of his grip and stood from the chair. "If I'm not back by the time you finish that," I said to Brea, pointing to what was left in her glass, "come find me."

"You know it." She raised her glass and took a drink, glaring at Reed as she swigged.

I held my wine as I led Reed to a back corner that was quieter than where Brea and I had been sitting, but close enough for her to see me. I couldn't imagine what he wanted to discuss. Our business matters had been handled; the last status report I'd read that morning showed that all pending contracts were being processed. And by the way he had treated me at the gala—comparing me to Julia, allowing her to degrade me without stepping in to defend me at all—I couldn't imagine he would have anything to say that was worth hearing.

I reached the corner and turned to face him. "What is it, Reed?"

"Frankie…" There was that look again—the look he had given me at the party right before I had left him and his too-late apology. The look that was full of sorrow…the look that did nothing but make me even angrier.

"It's been a long day and I really just want to enjoy my night with Brea, so say whatever it is you have to say." I didn't just want to enjoy my night; I wanted to forget so many things. Derek, and Reed, and the woman…and the scene I had walked in on in Reed's bedroom.

The blood.

"I'm sorry," he said quietly.

"You're sorry?" My eyes traced the deep lines in his forehead, the creases that surrounded his mouth as he frowned. He wasn't one to share his feelings. Maybe that had been part of our problem. Our issues had been shoved so far aside in favor of our jobs, we'd never let them surface long enough to discuss what was ruining our relationship until it was too late. Then there was nothing left to discuss. "Are you apologizing for the way you acted in front of Julia?" I didn't give him a chance to answer. "The least you could have done was have my back and put her in her place. But you didn't; you did nothing—no, worse than that, you gave her fuel to go further. I always knew you were selfish…but when did you become heartless?"

His hands ran through his hair and crossed over his chest. I could tell my words caused him pain. It was exactly what I wanted: to stir a reaction, to get him to feel something about how he'd treated me—regret, shame. Anything.

"I'm sorry for that, too," he said. He took a breath, his hands dropping to his sides. "Jesus, Frankie, I fucked up. All I've done is fuck up. What I said to you when I walked in on you and that developer was wrong." His eyes moved to my mouth. "I was jealous. I don't like the idea of you being with anyone but me. Seeing it was even worse than thinking about it."

"That's ironic, don't you think, considering what you were doing when I walked in on you…and *her*?" I wanted this day to be over, the memories of it to be erased as fast as the wine would allow.

He moved closer, resting against the wall. "She meant nothing to me."

"I don't care."

"It was a one night stand. I barely knew her name. I…"

I put my hand in his face. It was the only way to make him stop. "I don't care—about the details *or* your apology. I don't want to hear either."

"Then maybe you'll want to hear this instead: I miss you."

"Oh God." When I took a step back, his hand cuffed my wrist. "Reed, I can't do this."

"Let's go back to my place."

"No—"

"Your place, then. Somewhere not quite so loud or crowded, where we can have a conversation and not get interrupted." His free hand touched my cheek, his fingers brushing into my hair.

For just a second, I closed my eyes and breathed in his skin. I knew his touch, his voice; I knew he'd kiss me in the elevator as we rode up to my condo, take me by the hand and lead me to my bedroom. He'd strip off my clothes in front of the nightstand, hover above me as I lay on the mattress, and he'd fuck me until he shuddered. But there would be no passion, no lust, no longing so deep that my body would quiver for just the feel of his breath.

Reed wasn't who I wanted.

Even if I'd never been with Derek, never learned the depths of pleasure my body could reach, I still wouldn't have let Reed back in. He wasn't just part of my past; he was the greatest cause of my pain.

"I have to go."

"Frankie—"

I pulled my wrist out of his grip. "I can't breathe, I have to go…" I rushed away, and I stopped only when I reached Brea. I lifted my purse off the table, looping the strap over my shoulder. "This was a bad idea."

She set her phone down. "Coming here, or talking to him?" She was slurring her words even more, and so was I.

"Coming here, going out…all of it. I should be home, eating

more chocolate, sipping a glass of wine in my bathtub, not reopening wounds with Reed that neither of us can heal."

Even through her stupor, she looked concerned. "Time to go, hon."

I found my wallet inside my purse and dropped several bills on the table. It was more than enough to cover all the drinks. "Yes. It's definitely time."

She drank down the last of her wine. "Want me to come over?"

The waitress had delivered the shots of tequila while I'd been with Reed. I swallowed mine in one gulp, my mouth watering from the burn. "Thank you," I finally answered, "but I wouldn't make for good company. I need to be alone. We can share a cab, though, I'll drop you off on my way."

"No worries, it's only a few blocks. I'll walk."

She slung her bag over her shoulder, and I grabbed her hand as she stood. "You know I'm not going to let you walk."

Her eyes left mine. "Reed's coming back."

"Oh yeah…we're going."

I guided us through the crowd holding her hand, making our way quickly to the front of the bar. A cab was just pulling up outside, and a couple was getting out of the backseat. Brea and I slid in after them.

"Four blocks east, please, stop when you hit Boylston Street," Brea said to the driver.

"Sure thing," he said.

She relaxed into the seat, propping her purse onto her lap. "God, I'm way drunker than I thought."

I had realized the same thing as we were rushing through the bar. "Tell me we don't have an early meeting in the morning?"

"We don't…at least not anymore." She looked at me and grinned. "I had a feeling we were going to have more than a few glasses, so I postponed it until the afternoon."

"You're good."

She winked. "I know."

The cab driver pulled up to Boylston, putting on his blinker while he idled at the curb. She reached across to hug me. "You sure you want to be alone?"

"I'm sure. I'm just going to eat some more chocolate and go to bed."

I squeezed her for a second longer, then as I watched her walk into her building, I gave the driver my address. Once the taxi began moving again, I tucked myself into the corner of the backseat. I felt the weight of my phone inside my purse. If I took it out, I didn't know if I had the willpower to stop myself from texting Derek.

Anna had told me that survivors like her and I take risks. Derek was more than a risk. Ending things between us had made the most sense; I knew I couldn't keep things casual, I couldn't stop myself from getting attached, from falling in love. Seeing text messages from other women would destroy me. Knowing he'd been with others behind my back would make me hate him. And once I experienced that level of hurt again, I wouldn't want to work with him, and I would lose his contract.

Things may have been much harder this way, but they were also much safer.

"Fifteen dollars and forty-five cents," the driver said as he came to a stop in front of my building.

I handed him a twenty. "Keep it all. Thank you."

My doorman helped me out of the backseat. "You have a visitor waiting for you inside, Ms. Jordan."

"A visitor?"

Was it possible that Reed had gotten into a cab after us and had beaten me here?

He held out his arm, signaling me to walk in front of him. "I tried calling your cell and left you messages."

"Sorry about that," I said, holding the banister as I walked up the few stairs. I knew the heels were pinching my toes, but I could barely feel them. I could barely feel anything.

When he opened the lobby door, I immediately saw the visitor. He stood not far from the bank of elevators, his electric blue stare gazing back. Shivers exploded through my body as my eyes wandered over him. That beard, the one that made my folds pucker, and the mouth that made me scream, and the flannel that shackled my wrists to submission.

"Derek," I breathed, pausing in the middle of the lobby. Even this far away, it felt as if his lips were on me, his hands on my breasts, my body wrapped within his. "What the hell are you doing here?"

THREE.

DEREK

I saw the shock in her eyes at finding me standing in her lobby. She was right to be surprised; I never waited for anyone, especially a woman I had slept with. But this was the only way I could talk to her. She hadn't returned my calls, hadn't responded to my text. And Will had made just as much progress with Brea.

If Frankie was going to hide, then I was going to fucking

find her.

"You've been drinking," I said. She was walking toward the elevator, toward me, toward the tongue I wanted to plunge inside her. I could tell by the looseness in her body she'd had wine…the only other thing that could have made her that loose was my cock.

"I've had a few drinks," she replied.

"Is that why you've been missing since nine this morning? Because you've been drinking?"

"No."

"We need to talk. Now."

She glanced all around us. We were alone except for the doorman, and he was too far away to hear us. "We can talk here."

"Let's go to your condo."

She shook her head, holding herself up against the frame of the elevator. "No way."

I took a step closer so she could feel my breath, my need, the power in what I was telling her. "Once I say what I need to, I'll leave. I promise."

"Then you can say whatever you need to in this lobby. It's not like you've had a problem doing anything in public before."

That spicy goddamn mouth. She was fighting me, and although I would never tell her this, I fucking loved it. "I fingered your pussy in public…you're right about that." Goose bumps rose over her skin as my breath traveled down her neck. "But what I have to tell you isn't going to be said in this lobby."

Her eyes closed, her breathing sped up. Her teeth dug into her bottom lip. When her lids finally opened, she said, "Five minutes." She hit the button for the elevator. "That's all you get."

I followed her into the elevator, doing everything I could not to wrap my hands around her waist and devour her neck with my teeth. After seeing how my breath had affected her, I was certain I'd be touching her again. She was struggling with her feelings and trying to act strong. But if my hands went inside her panties, I knew her clit would be dripping with wetness and that warm, snug hole would be soaked.

She held onto the railing that wrapped around the middle of the elevator and stared at the numbers that lit up over the door. I was sure she did that to keep from looking at me. With each floor, I could see her mind spinning with questions; I could practically hear her pussy squealing with the need to be touched. She wanted, and she feared. She desired…and she regretted.

I knew, because I did, too.

We arrived at the penthouse, and she went straight to her kitchen and poured herself a glass of wine. She didn't bother to look in my direction. "I'd offer you one, but you won't be here long enough to drink it, so…"

That fiery fucking mouth was at it again. I wanted those lips pouted around my cock, humming from all the cum I was shooting down her throat. And I would get that, but first I needed to make things right.

I moved to the other side of the island. "It's been almost twelve hours since you were supposed to be at my townhouse. You have your voice and all your fingers, so why the hell didn't you reply to my calls or my text?"

She drank deeply. "I took a break from my phone today."

I tried to calm all the urges that were building within. I wasn't simply angry that she had blown me off; I was worried about her, too. "No breaks, Frankie. Not ever."

"I can do whatever the hell—"

"Let me finish." My sweet pink ivory was usually so submissive. She had never shown this much dominance. It made me want to smile, but I didn't want to give her that reaction. "When I call you, I don't care what time it is, I expect you to call me back. Text me back. Have Brea get in touch with me, if you need to. But I insist on an answer when I call. You're my realtor, Frankie, someone I trusted with my entire building—all one hundred and eighty-one units. It's my business, my livelihood, and my reputation on the line when you leave me hanging." Her face began to soften as the realization hit her. "We have a contract—a contract that every realtor in Boston wants right now—and it comes with clauses that allow me to terminate if I feel the agreement isn't being adhered to. Telling me you don't want to fuck me any more isn't a reason to do that, obviously, but ignoring me during business hours is."

Her eyes bounced from my face to the wine glass and back. That small gesture showed so much emotion. "I just needed a minute. I'm sorry."

I knew she was sorry. What I needed were answers, and I was going to get them. So I leaned into the counter, pushed my hands into the stone and demanded one. "Why did you leave my house this morning?"

Her brows rose, her back straightening. "So she told you I was there?"

"Of course Hayden told me…I was waiting for you, and you disappeared. So again, Frankie, why did you leave?"

"That was…Hayden?"

Why did it feel like I was missing something here? "Yes, that was Hayden."

She shook her head. While she was processing, it looked like she was filling with more hurt, more suffering.

I wanted to make it stop. "Frankie—"

"Why did you sleep with *her*?" It came out as a whisper, but a powerful one.

"With *Hayden*?" I laughed—a deep, honest, guttural laugh. Those gunmetal eyes were so large and fierce. She was confused and angry, and it all made her look so damn beautiful. I wanted to take all that frustration and make her whole body shake from the flicking of my tongue. "Baby—"

"Don't you dare laugh at me, Derek, and don't call me baby like a condescending prick. Our business meetings will take place in my office from now on, and you and I will never be alone again. Ever. Get out of my apartment."

I'd had enough.

I walked around the island; she backed up, her hands going into the air to stop me. "What the hell do you think you're doing?"

I was only inches away from her. She had nowhere to go. "I'm making sure you listen to me." I gripped the counter on both sides of her, my arms wedging her into me. "I don't know what you think happened, but it didn't."

"I know what I saw, you asshole. She—"

"Is my sister, Frankie." My voice lowered. "Hayden is my sister."

Her mouth fell open, and she gasped. "She's your…"

My actions were too quick; she didn't have enough time to respond or stop me before I ravaged her lips and made them mine. The fight, the resistance, the anger, the jealousy had all been the biggest turn-on. Finally having the taste of her in my mouth again made my balls ache, and my dick grow solid under my boxer briefs. When I felt her start to relax, the truth of my words finally setting in, I pulled away. "Yes," I said, licking her off my lip. "She's my sister."

FOUR.

FRANKIE

I halted as I processed Derek's statement...and the fact that his mouth had just been all over mine. "She's your sister?"

He hadn't had sex with her; she wasn't ruffled and messy because of him.

The thought repeated in my mind as the relief starting to spread. They were related, though.

I wasn't sure which was worse.

"You know her," he said. It wasn't a question; it was a statement, as if he already knew the answer. I wasn't sure I was ready to tell him exactly *how* I knew her. But I still wondered how close they were, how much he knew about his own sister.

"She told you?" I asked.

"She said she knew *of* you, but that doesn't explain why you left when you saw her. Now tell me how you know her."

I looked for my wine, but he had me caged so tightly I couldn't move. "Let's just say we have a past."

"Explain *your* past, then."

I felt his breath on my face. Minty, lustful, delicious. "I can't, Derek."

"Because you don't want to?"

"Exactly." His arms loosened and I wiggled my way out, taking my glass into the living room and sitting on the couch. I needed space, and a second to think. I needed to take a breath that wasn't full of him.

"I need a better reason than that, Frankie."

I closed my eyes and listened to his boots move across the wood floor of the kitchen, through the archway and into the living room. I felt him standing in front of me. "It's not just that I don't want to; it's also that she's your sister."

He sat on the far end of the couch and kept his hands on the cushions. His eyes searched my face. "Okay; I'll explain it, then. You left my house this morning because you took one look at Hayden and thought we were sleeping together. Then you avoided me all day. Is that close?"

"That's part of it, yes." I had made the decision to break things off with him. But after that kiss, it felt as though I had never uttered those words. The wine was making me far too honest.

"I worried about you all day, Frankie—that something had happened to you, that you were hurting somewhere…" His voice deepened. "Tell me the rest."

Either she had told him her side and he wanted to hear mine, or she hadn't told him anything and he wanted to hear it all from me. If he was pushing me this hard, I could only imagine he'd pushed her, too. "I found her in bed with Reed…while Reed and I were still dating. It ended our relationship. So, as you can probably guess, your sister isn't one of my favorite people." I didn't tell him everything.

Just enough to stop the questions.

"Fuck, he said.

I took a sip of my wine, feeling its warmth pass through my throat as it slowly moved toward my stomach. "I jumped to conclusions when I saw her at your townhouse, because I didn't know who she was to you. But there's too much pain that involves your sister, Derek, and I…" I had told her to fuck off; it all came back to me then. "…I acted out when I saw her. I said something I shouldn't have, and then I left. It wasn't the most mature reaction, but it was all I could do in that moment." I set the glass on the end table.

Derek leaned forward and ran his hand over my cheek, resting at my chin. "I didn't know about any of this. I'm sorry."

The smell of his skin was intoxicating, the scent I had craved when Reed's hands had been on me earlier: woods and body wash, a hint of cologne and all man. "You don't have to apologize for her."

"Yes, I do."

I shrugged. "If you have any other family members I should know about, now would be a good time to tell me."

His thumb brushed over my lip. "That fucking mouth." His growl reminded me of the sound that came from him just before he orgasmed. "Hayden is my only sibling."

I glanced down at my hands; they were fidgeting in my lap. His fingers were stirring feelings that were more intense than I wanted them to be. A yearning so deep, it made me want to grab his fingertips and place them on my nipple, to have him yank it so hard I'd scream. But I shouldn't have been thinking about his hands on my nipple, or his fingers anywhere near me. They should have been in his lap like mine were…because nothing could happen between us anymore.

I looked at him again, reminding myself that we were having a conversation about his sister, not his fingers, or where I wanted them on my body. He'd apologized for something that wasn't his fault. I owed him something similar. "I'm sorry for making an unqualified assumption, and for avoiding you all day because of it. It was wrong of me."

"Now that I know the truth, I'm glad it happened. It shows me how much you care."

But I wasn't supposed to care, was I? And neither was he. That was what we'd agreed to: business only. Our encounters had been incredible mistakes that would never be made again.

I glanced away, unwilling to meet his eyes. If I did, he'd see the truth, which I was sure he could already feel in my body, hear in my voice, sense in my posture. But my eyes would confirm it, without question. I had told him we needed to end things, and I needed to stick with that, to stay strong.

"Look at me."

He was inside my head again, responding as if I were speaking my thoughts aloud.

"I can't."

I felt him stand from the couch and move around to the front of me. Then his hands were under my arms, lifting me off the cushion and wrapping me around his waist. "Look at me, Frankie."

"I—"

"Look at me."

He wasn't going to give up until I gave him what he wanted, and from this position, I couldn't avoid him forever. Slowly, I raised my eyes and met his gaze. I felt it in every part of my body. If looks could devour flesh, his did that to me. His mouth parted and he sighed over my face.

"Fuck…I want you."

I wasn't sure which one of us had said that, but I felt like it had come from me.

FIVE.

DEREK

Her body was speaking to me, telling me exactly what I wanted to hear. But her mind was holding her back. There was fear in her eyes. She wasn't afraid of me; she was afraid of what would happen between us, what would come of us professionally if things didn't work out personally. I understood that. Before her, I'd never craved a woman longer than the hours my cock had been sunk inside her. Frankie broke every single rule I'd set, every promise.

How could I ever give a woman more than just the one night and one morning? Hell if I knew. But I knew I wanted something more with her, something I couldn't define. The desire for it was there, and that was enough for now.

I didn't think I could let go even if she wanted me to. Her ass was resting on my palms; her heels dug into my lower back as her hands gripped my shoulders. It all felt perfect.

So fucking perfect.

"I'm giving you a chance to change your answer," I said.

She ran her fingers over my beard. I knew then what she was going to say, but I let the moments of silence pass between us, allowing her to feel like she had some control. The second I dipped inside her panties, which we were just moments away from, her control would be gone.

"Derek, I…" I stared at her lips, watching how they moved when she spoke my name, how they remained open when she paused and no sound came out. She was so beautiful, so raw, trying so hard to be strong after telling me about Hayden. It hadn't been easy for her. I wanted her to feel like she could trust me with more than just her body, even if that truth involved my sister.

"If you want me, if you want this, then you have to tell me. And it has to be now." I looked at her wrist. The bracelet she knew I liked was wrapped around her delicate skin; it was the one I had once asked her to wear. She had worn it today and that told me everything I needed to know. "Because Frankie, I don't believe you really want things between us to end." Her cheeks darkened and her pupils began to dilate with need. "If you tell me you don't want me, I'll…" She had to know I would respect her despite what I wanted. "…I'll put you down and I'll leave your condo. What happened between us won't affect what we have professionally. I promise. But if you want me, then—"

Her fingers clenched my whiskers and pulled me toward her; her lips crashed against mine, her tongue teasing its way into my mouth. She moaned as I tightened my grip on her ass, lowering her enough to grind her against my dick. My cock was so fucking hard; it was begging to be let out of my jeans and plunged into the sopping wetness that I knew was waiting for me.

I was done waiting.

I carried her to the kitchen and sat her on top of the island, on the same stone slab that had separated us earlier. I dug out my wallet and grabbed the condom I kept in there.

Those gunmetal eyes were so passionate, so demanding as I held the foil between my fingers. "Fuck me," she begged, her command making my dick throb even harder.

"I'm going to reward you for saying that."

"Please, Derek. I want you now."

I unbuttoned her pants and yanked them off, and did the same with her panties, but left her heels on. Then I unbuttoned my jeans and dropped them just far enough to free my cock. I tore open the foil and rolled on the condom before I pulled her to the edge of the counter. "Put your hands around my neck and don't let go." She obeyed my order. "I don't care how good it feels, you are not to move your hands—do you understand me?"

"Yes," she moaned. Her lips were on my cheek, traveling toward my ear.

My dick rubbed against her thigh as I caressed her clit. She was more than ready—wet, warm, tight, and hardening under my touch. As much as I wanted her, I didn't want to hurt her. So I drove two fingers into her pussy, opening her wide enough to fit my dick. Her cunt curved around me, her grunting vibrating against my chest as her fingers clasped my shoulders. "Does that feel good, baby?"

She leaned her head back and opened her eyes. The city lights shone across her face the same way they had in the hotel room. She was fucking delicious.

She ran her tongue over her bottom lip. "Yes…it feels *sooo* good."

"Are you ready for me?"

She nodded, and I slowly pulled my fingers out. I moved closer and eased my tip into her. "You're so goddamn tight," I hissed.

Her legs squeezed around me. "Let me feel you, Derek."

I rocked my hips forward and sunk into her. Her pussy was so warm and so snug, it practically clutched me when I banged my balls against her.

"Oh my God," she yelled. "Don't stop."

I held her face and forced her eyes open. "Tell me what

you want."

"This—"

"No, Frankie." I kissed her quickly, reminding her of the claim I had on her mouth, on her body, on the pussy I was buried deep inside. "Tell me what you want."

She glanced at me sidelong, her eyes slowly closing. "You, Derek. I just want you."

I wrapped my hands under her ass and lifted her off the counter. As her heels rubbed the back of my thighs, urging me to give her more, I hissed across her cheek. "You're going to get me. All of me. All night long."

"I hope so," she moaned. She tipped her head to the left. "My room is that way."

"Fuck the bedroom."

"Good, I'm sick of it."

I kicked off my jeans and moved through the living room, driving into her with each step, searching for a wall that had nothing hanging on it. When I found one, I pushed her against it and used my weight to hold her there. Squeezing her ass, spanking it with just the tips of my fingers, I plunged in and out of her hole.

"Kiss me," I demanded. My other hand roamed her body until I found her tit, then with each thrust, I squeezed her nipple, pulling it through her shirt and the lace of her bra. Her back arched, her heels now puncturing my ass. The points felt like blades, which only made me fuck her harder.

"Oh…" she breathed, "my…" she grunted, "…GOD!" she yelled. She tightened around me as I pulled out, pausing at the tip of my cock before shoving all the way back in.

"I know you want to come."

"Yes…God, yes." Her nails dug into me now too, stabbing my neck as she clutched tighter. "I don't know how much longer I can hold off…"

I rocked forward, thrusting again and again. My balls tightened as I tried to keep from shooting my load. "Come with me, Frankie."

"Now?"

"Yes—right fucking *now*."

I waited for her body to shudder, for her pussy to contract, for her screaming to fill my ears before I let go and emptied every bit of my cum. Her heels dropped as her arms went limp, but her hands remained around my neck. She didn't want to let go…and I hadn't told her she was allowed to.

"I don't know how you do that," she said as she finally stilled.

"Do what?"

"Make my body feel the way that you do."

"Your own fingers can't do the same thing?" I knew the answer I just wanted to hear her say it.

She straightened and lifted her head away from the wall. My lips found her neck, her vein, her pulse speeding up, tapping against my mouth. "No, not even close."

I pulled back and read her eyes. "You touched yourself, didn't you? After I told you not to."

The corners of her lips curved down, and her nose scrunched up. That told me everything I needed to know.

"You were warned," I growled.

"In my defense, I had broken things off with you. So technically, I was allowed to touch myself whenever I wanted." While I carried her down the hall, she nuzzled her face into my neck, her tongue darting over the skin she'd clawed just moments before. Her lips then caressed it. "Am I being punished for it?"

I reached the room at the end of the hall and turned on the light. "Yours?" I confirmed.

"Mmmhmm."

I passed a large walk-in closet and continued on until I reached the bathroom. I tried all the switches near the door until I found one that controlled the recessed pin lights, which gave the room a faint glow.

Stopping near the tub, I leaned her back so I could look at her face. "Fuck…I can't get enough of you, my pink ivory." I'd wondered all day if I'd ever be able to call her that again, if I'd ever hold this perfect ass or feel her soft, wet flesh wrapped tightly around my dick. And now I had her back—this dangerous, gorgeous woman who had changed me, who had made me do things I never thought I would.

Who made me feel things I'd never intended on feeling.

"So have me again," she said. "And again after that."

"No demands. You'll get what I give you." I set her on the marble bench inside the walk-in shower and turned on the water. While I waited for it to warm, I pulled off her shirt, unclasped her bra and got her fully naked.

"Aren't you going to join me?" She stuck her foot under the stream.

I watched the way the water ran along her shin, how it coursed over her feet when she rubbed them together. I imagined how it would taste when mixed with the flavor of her skin.

I couldn't wait one more goddamn second.

Quickly flushing the used condom, I then dropped my clothes on the floor and stepped into the shower. After pulling her off the bench, she joined me under the waterfall head, the side jets that were mounted into the wall sprayed over the top and bottom half of our bodies. It was a shower that transformed into a steam room, built for someone who didn't just use it to wash, but someone who needed to relax too. I had constructed one very similar in my house in Portsmouth.

Frankie's skin was glossy from the stream, her delicate neck fully exposed, her hungry fingers running through her hair…fingers I wanted clamped around my cock. She was decadent. Vulnerable. It took almost every ounce of self-control I had not to spread her legs and plunge my bare dick inside her.

The body wash I squeezed into my hand smelled like the beach and I massaged it over her. I rubbed small circles around her tits, her nipples hardening on my palms. I dipped my face, brushing my beard over each one.

"*Ohhhh*," she moaned, panting. "That feels so good." Her hands went to my chest and slid down my abs and slowly moved back up my sides. Starting just below my armpit, she traced the black scripted letters that were tattooed over my ribs, ending at the side of my waist. "White," she said, reading the ink.

It had been on my skin for so long, some days I forgot it was there. But when I was reminded, it reinforced what I needed to do, what Hayden and I needed to accomplish. It was my outer-most layer, hardened like bark to protect the rings within.

It was more than my protection.

It was *me*.

"It's an odd word to have permanently written on your body." My eyes followed her fingers. "What does it mean?

Maybe I would tell her one day. I'd let her into that part of my life and explain what had happened to my family and how I planned to make it right. But not today. "It's my favorite color."

She laughed, the sound echoing off the stone and glass, loosening her body even more in my hands. "For some reason, I don't believe you."

"No?" I kept working those small buds between my thumb and pointer finger, pulling and teasing, getting them ready for my teeth.

"No," she sighed as pleasure spread over her face. "Your favorite color is in the beige family—natural, earthy and woodsy like your architecture…like your passion." She chewed the corner of her lip. "Either that, or whatever color lingerie I happen to be wearing when you take it off with your teeth. But it's definitely not white."

That description…I wanted to taste it.

I grabbed her ass, pulling her against me as I took her mouth again. While she sucked the end of my tongue, I lifted her into the air, sat her on top of the bench and kneeled in front of her. Then I spread her legs as wide as they could go and buried my face between them.

"*Ahhhhh*," she moaned, her thighs closing in on my cheeks. "Derek, your tongue…"

I looked up at her, my lapping coming to a stop. "What about my tongue?"

"Don't…fucking…stop."

I flicked it again, slower this time, taunting her with it. "Remember that punishment you asked about?"

"Oh God…no."

"This," and I lapped her clit, "is going to continue for a long time."

"And what constitutes a long time?" She closed her legs again, but I pushed them apart. Her back arched as more moaning escaped from her lips.

I licked her again. "When you're screaming so loudly to come, and your whole body is shaking with need, and you can't take another second of it."

"And then?"

"Then…" I dove back in, feeling how close she was getting as her pussy closed in around my fingers, her clit hardening under my tongue. "…and only then…" I tilted them up toward her G-spot and let her feel both sensations before I paused. "…will I reward you."

"But…but I can't take much more," she panted.

I smiled. The look of pleasure and frustration that crossed her face was so beautiful. "Yes, you can, Frankie. And you will."

SIX.

FRANKIE

I woke up to pounding. It was louder than just a regular knock; it was a fist hammering against my front door. I checked the time on my phone and found it was a few minutes past six.

I gently lifted the blanket, trying not to wake Derek as I grabbed a robe from the bathroom and shut the bedroom door. I looked through the peephole and saw Reed. What the hell was he doing here? It was shocking enough to wake me fully.

"Frankie?" He knocked again. "The doorman said you

haven't left for work yet. I know you're in there."

I considered remaining silent, but I wanted him gone. "It's…not a good time, Reed."

"Just open the door."

I knew he wasn't going to go away until I let him in. But how had he gotten up here? I remembered the list that the front desk kept on file of the people who were sent straight up to my condo without the doorman calling me first. Anna, Brea, and my father were on there, but I thought I'd taken Reed off after we'd broken up. I was furious with myself for forgetting to do it.

I opened the door just a crack and looked through the gap. "I'm not dressed." But Reed was—fully showered, shaved, and holding two coffees in his hands. His cologne tickled my nose like a room full of dust.

"It's nothing I haven't seen." He slipped his hand through the narrow opening and pushed it wider, giving himself enough room to move inside.

"Reed, you can't just barge your way in here."

He slid in past me, stopping when he reached the living room. He placed the coffees on the table. "You left last night before I could—"

"Frankie…"

Our heads swiveled toward my bedroom, where Derek stood in the archway wearing a pair of jeans…and nothing else. My eyes ran over his hard chest and the bottom of the tattooed letters that peeked out from under his arm. He was the sexiest man I had ever been with; it was all the more obvious with Reed being so close by for contrast. I slowly looked over at my ex. His jaw flexed as he ground his teeth.

"Are you okay?" Derek asked me.

"You don't have to check on her, asshole." Reed's voice was starting to rise. "I can handle her just fine."

"Frankie…" Derek demanded.

I kept an eye on Reed to make sure this didn't go any further. "Yes. I'm fine."

"What is *he* doing here?" Reed asked me.

"What are *you* doing here?" Derek asked him back.

"Listen asshole, she's my—"

"That's the second time you've called me an asshole this morning," Derek said, his voice eerily calm, but extremely firm. He moved closer to us. "I let it pass the first time, I won't the—"

I slid between the two men, keeping closer to Derek and his amazing body. "Stop it," I insisted. "Both of you."

Reed pointed at Derek. "Is this why you left the bar last night? To be with that?"

Derek crossed his arms over his chest and laughed.

"Reed," I said, not bothering to dignify his comment, "it's time for you to go."

"Are you really asking me to leave?"

I nodded.

The muscles in Derek's chest tightened as his hands dropped and clenched at his sides. "Take your smug-ass grin and get the fuck out of here," Derek said.

"You're nothing," Reed yelled.

"Maybe to you I'm nothing, but I'm the nothing who has command of Frankie's attention, and much more than just that. I'm not the one who shows up the morning after…I'm the one who was invited the night before."

"That can't be—"

"Ask her if you don't believe me."

Heat filled my face as both men stared at me. The tension in this room was becoming too much. An ugly web had been woven, based on lies, betrayal and blood, and I was at its center. I wanted it all to come to an end.

"When she realizes who's best for her—and she will realize that—she'll come to me willingly. No commands necessary," Reed said.

Derek's smile fell away. "Will she catch you in bed with another woman this time, too?"

There it was: the question I had feared, about the subject I dreaded. I knew how vulgar Derek could be, how many different ways he could have worded it. His sister was involved, so he'd kept it clean. But his anger at Reed was so apparent.

Shock and fury washed over Reed's face. I believed it was from knowing that I'd told Derek about our situation. I hoped there might be a little guilt in there, too.

"Keep the coffee," Reed told me. "It's your favorite, made just the way you like it, something I doubt he'd bother to learn about you." He turned and stalked to the front door. "We're not finished, Frankie. And Derek…neither are we." Then he slammed it behind him.

I tightened my robe and dropped onto the couch, staring at the coffees and thinking about what had just taken place. As much as I tried, I couldn't stop my hands from shaking.

"That shouldn't have happened," Derek said. He sat next to me and wrapped his arm around my shoulders. "I'm sorry."

It shouldn't have happened—not first thing in the morning before I'd had a chance to even know what was going on, and certainly not while things between Derek and me were still so undefined.

I folded my arms over my stomach and looked at him. "What are you sorry for?"

"I'm sorry for losing my temper, and that you had to hear all that…that you felt like you had to put yourself in the middle of it."

"I am in the middle of it, Derek." Of what, I had no idea, but it was definitely me standing between the two of them.

"Let me finish, Frankie." He tucked a chunk of my hair behind my ear. "I know now what that bastard represents to you. I wish he hadn't showed up to make trouble, but I'm glad I was here when he did, because had he touched you…" He paused, his expression full of rage, "I wouldn't be sorry for what I would have done to him. I know that doesn't make it easier for you…and neither does embarrassing you, but I couldn't stop myself from putting him in his place."

There was something bothering me even more than all of that.

"You said you've got a hell of a lot more than just the command of my attention," I reminded him. "What exactly do you mean by that?"

His brows furrowed. "I mean that I hope I'm more important to you than he is at this point." He was. Much more important. But I didn't have to give him that answer because he immediately asked another question. "How often does he show up here unannounced?"

"Almost never. I saw him last night at the bar that Brea and I were at. He asked to come home with me so we could talk. That obviously didn't happen, and I left without saying good-bye. And because I've been so preoccupied with you, I haven't returned any of his calls...apparently, there have been several." There were more than that, actually...more than fifteen as of this morning. "He must have come over because he was worried."

Derek scoffed. "He doesn't need to worry."

"Okay."

"You're fine, and I will make sure you stay that way."

"I don't need to be taken care of, Derek." I tucked my legs into my chest and wrapped my arms around them. As nerve-wracking as it was, I wanted him to tell me what was happening between us. I knew how I felt, and how it had started to change, but I couldn't be constantly wondering if he was feeling the same. "You've got to give me something."

"No, you don't need to be taken care of, Frankie, but I want to." His eyes narrowed. "As for giving you something, I think I gave you a lot of me last night."

"You did," I agreed. "But I need more than your tongue, or your dick."

I watched him as he thought about my question. I imagined the things he wanted to say, that he was holding back because of the distance he was trying to keep.

"Our night at the hotel was different for me," he said finally.

"Different how?"

"This..." He ran his fingers over my cheek, along my mouth and into my hair. He combed the strands and tugged at the ends. "This is different, too—me being here. Spending more time with you. It doesn't happen this way. Ever."

Having a second night with me was rare for him. As rare as me having any night at all with him. I wasn't the only one who had built a box around myself.

Block. It was fitting.

"Then tell me what that means," I said.

"It means I want more of you."

I took a deep breath. "How much more?"

His eyes didn't give me an answer either. "More."

"More...okay."

"Just okay?"

"I..." My voice trailed off; I didn't know how much I would allow myself to say. This part, I wasn't good at. I struggled with sharing my feelings. It had been easier to push Derek away after our night at the hotel than it was to answer this simple question because nothing about my emotions were simple or easy to verbalize.

But his eyes demanded an answer.

And I wanted to give him that, to be truthful. But the words weren't there. I felt them; I knew they existed somewhere within me. But it was too hard to say them.

My silence lasted too long.

He stood from the couch, bent down to lift me, and threw me over his shoulder. "Derek!" I squealed, his firm muscle pushing into my stomach. "Where are you taking me?" I felt so light, so small against his sizable frame.

"I'm getting what I want out of you."

I clutched his back to keep from sliding. "And what is that?"

"A goddamn answer."

SEVEN.

DEREK

Frankie didn't purge her desire like Julia, or whine about her need like Tamra. She locked up like a goddamn vise. That was something I understood; it was what I had done since ending things with my ex all those years ago. Ending...more like her running off, which was equally painful. But understanding Frankie's silence didn't mean I was going to accept it. If this thing between us—whatever the hell this was—was going to work, she would need to tell me what was happening inside her.

And if she wasn't going to answer my question willingly, then my tongue was going to make her talk.

I threw her on top of the bed, pulling the string that held her robe together and spread it open to reveal her naked body. Then I knelt on the floor and yanked her toward the end of the mattress until her pussy met my mouth.

"*Ooooo…*" she moaned as I blew over her clit.

"Tell me what you want from me, Frankie."

She squeezed the blanket in her hands. "I want your tongue."

"You'll get it." I licked her quickly. Then I stuck the tip of my tongue into her hole, driving it into her again and again before I dragged it all the way up to her clit. "But if you want more than this, you have to tell me how you feel."

"I feel incredible."

"Now tell me how you feel when my tongue isn't inside you."

Her toes curled around the edge of the mattress. "I…can't."

My finger ran up and down her clit. I stuck it inside her—not deep, just up to the first knuckle. I felt her tightness, the warmth that I wanted my dick to be sunk into. Then I pulled it out, and she released a long, deep exhale. "Then tell me how you feel when it *is* inside you."

"Desired."

"And?" I brushed her clit.

"Insatiable."

"And?" I did it again.

"Extremely obedient."

It was no secret I was teasing her into admitting that. She enjoyed my tongue whenever I gave it to her, and I would make sure she enjoyed it again—but not until she submitted to me. And not just with her body.

I wanted all of her now.

I dove back in, flicking her clit from side to side. She clenched her fists and pulled at the blanket, her knees bending and straightening.

"How does my presence make you feel, Frankie?"

She looked at me as I gazed up from between her legs. "Different." Her eyes closed and her head tilted back as I gave her another lick.

"Different how?" I asked.

"Different from how I felt with Reed…" I inserted my finger all the way, circling inside her and pulling out. "…different from how I've felt with anyone."

I pointed my tongue again and brushed it over the length of her clit. I felt no relief when I ate her pussy, but watching her body build and buck at the constant flicking of my tongue was so fucking delicious that it was almost as good as coming.

"When I'm…" She paused. She was trying, I had to give her credit for that. My tongue had been on her for minutes, and she was still fighting against giving me an answer. "When I'm not with you, I want to be," she said finally. She pushed her legs together to urge more movement from me. I forced them apart…and gave her none. "I care, Derek." She angled up on her elbows, her body as restless as her mind. My mouth was making things even worse for her. "I care about you."

"Then tell me what you want, Frankie." I held her thighs open, but kept my face several inches back and locked eyes with hers so she could see me, take all of me in. So she would know exactly what she was getting when she finally said it out loud.

"I want more of this." She slid her legs down on the bed, curled them over the edge of the mattress, and rubbed her hands over her thighs. "More of you."

I didn't know how this would work. I wasn't used to anything beyond one night, one morning with a woman, and I certainly wasn't used to having an attachment that couldn't be resolved with my dick. But I knew I cared, too. And I felt the same as she did: desired, insatiable. It was so fucked up. And the most fucked up thing of all?

I felt full when she was in my arms.

I took her face in my palms and pulled her to me, and I gave those lips everything they deserved. She relaxed under my grip—melted, even. She allowed me to take her face as close as I could get it, even with my whiskers scratching her skin.

She didn't pull away. She didn't balk.

There were emotions, words, explanations she couldn't express yet. I had to give her something in return. I had to give her something more than my body. "I want more, too," I told her. "Much more."

I released her face, dropped back between her thighs and brought her pussy to my mouth. There was no fingering this time, no probing her hole with my tongue. All I did was lick, because it made her feel incredible, and making her feel that good made me feel powerful. It was easier for me than speaking, or sharing, or admitting. I knew how to take care of a pussy, and I was excellent at it. The other stuff—relationships, emotions, opening up and making myself vulnerable—I was shit at.

When Frankie moaned that she was close, I licked faster; when her back arched off the bed and her hands reached for me, I licked harder. When she asked me if she could come, I slowed down and only flicked with the tiniest point of my tongue. It was enough to keep her there, but not enough to send her over the edge. Once we passed that point, there would be a chance for her to ask questions and make demands—the same as I'd done to her.

I wanted none of that.

I wanted more of her pussy, more of her grunting. I wanted a whole lot more of her fucking wetness. So that was where I stayed, avoiding the bridge we were crossing. And everything else—the begging to come, the quivering in her navel as she neared—was just a reminder that my tongue was suited for one thing, and one thing only.

EIGHT.

FRANKIE

"Girl, you're seriously glowing," Brea said, her fork hovering over her salad. We had just finished a showing and had stopped for lunch on our way back to the office. "Whatever he's doing to you, he'd better not stop."

A wave of heat passed over my chest. "I hope you're the only one who can see that."

"Why?"

"I don't want my sex life written all over my face. It wouldn't be good for business, and it wouldn't look good in front of my father either."

She tilted her head back and laughed, showing me a mouthful of carrot. "It's far too late for that." Then she dipped her fork in for another bite. "I can see the multiple orgasms all over you, and the redness on your chin from grinding it into the mattress." I felt my cheeks blush as she glanced at my hands. "And where he bound your wrists…"

"Oh God." I touched my chin, feeling for a mark. I didn't find anything, so I checked my wrists, moving the bracelet I wore on the right and the Rolex on the left. There were no marks on either, which meant there was no way she could know. "You're just messing with me, aren't you?"

"Of course I am." She watched me closely. "But I'm right, obviously…you *freak*!" She let out a noise that was a mix of a sigh and a moan. "Explain something to me: how were you able to get ready for work this morning?"

"How?" I was confused by her question. "Well, I got up, and took a shower…" That had been the first shower I had taken alone since Derek had come over. The other two had been much more memorable. During the first, his tongue had teased me to an orgasm, and the second we'd had sex against the stone wall. "Then I straightened my hair and found something to wear."

"No, I mean how did you leave him this morning? If Mr. Block were in my bed, I'd be calling in sick to work. Every day."

She'd been encouraging my involvement with Derek since the day she'd witnessed our chemistry, and I appreciated that. But her comment was exactly what I'd feared all along. There were moments last night when Derek was covered in me—his hands, his mouth, his dick. Those had been the only things that had mattered. And to be truthful, I had contemplated calling in sick, asking Brea to take my clients to the scheduled showing, and staying in bed all day. If he hadn't gotten up before me to meet with Will, I might have tried to convince him to do the same.

I couldn't make sense of it, or of myself—the voracious sexual deviant I had become.

Running Jordan International wasn't just a career goal or a family business birth right; it was a desire so strong, so motivating, there were times I could think of nothing else.

My father may have been the controller and the face of the company, but I was the mortar that held it all together. It wasn't only him depending on me; it was Brea too, and our team of over one hundred agents, plus all the office staff. But my feelings for Derek were starting to trump my professional passion. I wondered how I had let it happen, and how I would make it stop, or at least slow it down so I could get a grip on both.

"Frankie?"

I glanced up when I heard my name. I had been staring blankly at my wrists. "Yes?"

Brea was glaring at me. "So why are you here with me instead of there with him?"

I grabbed my glass and swallowed half the water in it. "Derek had a meeting, so he left before me."

She leaned in and wrapped her fingers around my hand. "He hasn't put a ring on it. Relax. You're just having some fun. There's nothing wrong with that."

The waitress appeared with a pitcher of water and refilled my glass. "Can I get you ladies anything else?"

"A bottle of pinot noir, please," I said.

"With two glasses?"

"Yes, thank you."

"I'll bring that right out," she said and left our table.

My attention turned back to Brea. "I forgot to ask, do we have more showings this afternoon?"

She shook her head. "We have a conference call in a little bit. Then there's a closing downstairs that you need to stop by, and a traffic meeting after that. You'll be fine. And honestly, if you hadn't ordered the wine, I was going to."

"The closing isn't with Reed, is it?"

"There's no broker. It's a cash sale."

Relief passed through me. "That's good news." I couldn't take any more Reed at the moment. I definitely needed to discuss his showing up unexpectedly and barging into my home. That conversation would inevitably lead to the one we'd never had…about the future we would never have together. Once I found him with Hayden, everything between us had been thrown up in the air. Only our business relationship had landed intact. We needed to talk about all of it, and we would. I just wasn't ready for that conversation yet.

The screen of my phone lit up with an email, a note from the assistant of the international client to whom I'd shown several units last week.

"Something good?" Brea asked.

"Fernando wants to buy two units at Timber Towers. One of the penthouses for himself, and a unit on a lower floor as an investment. He wants me to put together a written offer for both."

"What does he want to pay?"

I continued to skim the email. "Full price for the penthouse; twenty-thousand under asking for the second unit."

"Damn…Mr. Block will be impressed."

"I think it will take more than two offers to impress him, but I do think it's a good sign of what's to come."

"None of the units are even on the MLS yet and the first person you show the pocket listing to wants to submit a contract that's worth over five million. Yeah, I'd say this is definitely a good sign."

I sent Derek a text:

Me: I'll be submitting two offers later today. Same buyer. Includes a penthouse. Thought you'd want to know.

I looked up just as the waitress returned with our wine. After she filled our glasses, Brea held hers up in the air. "Should we toast to the first offer?"

I smiled. "I think that's appropriate."

"To two down, one hundred and seventy-nine more to go!" Our glasses clinked.

I knew the units would start moving fast once we held the

brokers open, and they were all listed on the MLS. Derek didn't have much competition in the new construction arena. Maybe then our relationship would make more sense because he would no longer be a client.

"To that," I said.

"And to Mr. Block's dick, for turning you into a smiling fool and making you the happiest I've ever seen you."

I almost choked. "I can't believe we're toasting to *that*."

"It's not just a *that;* it's a dick, and they're important." We laughed. "And it's not just any dick; it's Mr. Block's dick."

My skin flushed as I thought of how I'd referred to him as Mr. Block and the punishment he'd doled out. I'd screamed for more of his tongue, his fingers…of him. I'd enjoyed it more than he probably intended. "Mr. Block…"

"No. Mr. Block's *dick*."

I rolled my eyes. "Yes, I got that part."

"Say it with me, Frankie: Dick. Dick. Dick. It's like: Orgasm. Orgasm. Orgasm. They go hand in hand…or dick in hand. You get the point."

"You're too much…" my voice trailed off as Derek's name appeared on the screen of my phone:

Derek: *You're so fucking sexy when you talk business. As sexy as when you talk about my cock and tell me how badly you want it and how hard you want me to fuck you with it.*

I couldn't escape the dick talk. It didn't matter. Even if Brea hadn't brought it up, even if I wasn't hearing it or reading it, I was thinking about it. Wanting it. Craving it more than I should have been during a business lunch.

"He's texting you, isn't he?" She leaned into the table and tried to peek at my phone.

"He is." I took a sip of my wine.

"Is he talking about his dick, too? He should be. EVERYONE should be. "

I felt the blush rise again. "No, he isn't."

"Liar. I can see it all over your face." She tore off the

corner of her bread and threw it at me. "Not only have you found a man who actually knows how to use his dick and one that can give you multiple orgasms, but you've found someone who likes to talk about it, too." Her face was glowing. "He's dirty. And you know I like 'em dirty. Jesus, Frankie, I'm officially jealous." She stood quickly and I thought she was going to come to my side of the table and read what he'd written. She took a few steps instead and looked at me over her shoulder. "I'm going to the ladies. Don't get crazy while I'm gone—that means keeping your hands above the tablecloth *at all times.*"

"Brea!" I gasped.

She winked and walked away.

I looked back at my phone and typed a reply:

Me: I want it. When am I getting more of it?
Derek: Tonight. Dinner. Then I get to eat you.

Derek was used to getting everything he wanted. He wasn't used to being challenged. Something told me he'd want me even more if I resisted a little.

Me: I'm not sure if I'm free. Give me a little bit and I'll check my schedule.
Derek: Make yourself free.
Me: I'll see what I can do.
Derek: The Hole. 7:00. No exceptions.

I smiled as I slipped my phone into my purse.

NINE.

DEREK

I had twenty minutes before I had to meet Frankie at The Hole. Twenty minutes until I got to taste those perfect lips and run my hands over that phenomenal body. I'd been thinking about her all afternoon. Fuck...I'd been thinking about her since the moment I left her condo. But issues had arisen at the jobsite today—problems with the plumbing, wrong electrical switches had been ordered, paint that came in a few shades too dark. Her texts had made it better, made it all feel insignificant. Not just the thought of having her tonight, but the thought of her, of Frankie.

The one I was supposed to stay away from, and the one I couldn't get enough of now.

My cock had been hard almost all day—from her texts, from teasing me about dinner and not agreeing until a few hours ago, from the thought of what would happen afterward. Her lack of submission made me want to drive to her office and fuck her on her desk.

Dinner was going to be a short one.

I turned off my computer and grabbed my bag. Before I could make it past my desk, Will came into my office. "You're not going to like what I'm about to tell you."

"If it's going to cause me to be late, then you're right."

"Randy's here. He's in the lobby and wants to speak with you. Security is with him, and they're going to escort him out, but I wanted to tell you before they do."

"Motherfucker." I slammed my bag down on top of the desk. "What does he want?"

"He wouldn't say. He just asked to speak with you… insisted, actually." Will stepped back into the hallway. "We've been waiting for this. I'm surprised it took him this long to come here."

I caught up to him and we walked to the lobby. "He couldn't have picked a worse night."

Randy stood near the front entrance, with security guards on both sides of him. He looked grayer, older. Beaten from exhaustion. More haggard than he had at the gala, or maybe the patio had just lacked good lighting.

Will and I stopped several feet away. My fists wouldn't be able to reach him unless I took a few steps. "You got me here, now what do you want?"

There was always a look of confidence on his face, and I never knew why. The man had nothing—no family, no friends, not even a decent amount of success. All he had was a new piece of land in Hull that wasn't worth what he was paying for it, a track record of shady deals, and a realtor who liked to suck my cock.

He shoved his hands into his jeans, spreading his feet

apart. "I want a tour of Timber Towers, son."

I laughed so hard, my throat went dry. "You want a tour? Of my building?"

"You followed me to Boston, so I want a goddamn tour of the building that you think is so much better than mine." He glared at the security guard when he clamped his hand around Randy's arm.

My building *was* better than his—all of them were, as were my residential homes. Hell, even the storage shed I had built behind my house was more sound than the shit he called quality construction. He cut corners; he used cheap materials. He barely met code. I didn't know why anyone would ever buy from him. But the fact that he sold his units didn't bother me as much as his total disregard for the poor, innocent bastards he employed and the conditions they worked in. They deserved better...I knew that first-hand.

"You don't want a tour, Randy." He didn't flinch. "So why did you really come here?" I felt the guard's eyes on my face, waiting for my signal to drag him out—or to hold him steady while I knocked him out. One of the two would eventually happen if this visit lasted much longer.

"I came to warn you." His jaw jutted out. He looked like a bulldog with a severe underbite. "Stay away from my land, son. I don't know what you're up to, and I don't know what you've got planned, but I don't like it one bit."

I didn't know how he'd gotten the information that I'd been looking into his land. Tamra wouldn't have been the one to tell him; I was sure she was still loyal to me, and would stay that way. I just needed to wean her completely off my dick and double-up on her pay.

"You're not my concern, and you never have been," I informed him. "So stop worrying about what I'm doing and start focusing on the people you *should* be worrying about."

"For some reason, I don't think you're being honest with me."

"What is it that you think I want, Randy?"

He shrugged, but the answer was clear in his eyes. "My

money. My power."

Laughing again would only prove him right. And he wasn't right—not even close. "I have my own money and my own power."

"No, son. What you have is a whole lot of investors who fund your buildings and a pretty, long-legged agent running around town shouting your name against every investor's cock she sticks in her mouth."

My hands balled into fists and I took a step forward. Will was immediately at my side, holding me back. There was no way I was going to let him talk about Frankie that way. But if I showed him Frankie was a weakness, she would become his focus, and I couldn't let that happen either.

"That ain't power," he continued. "That ain't shit, really. No one cares about green and natural elements and all that rubbish you like to flaunt. This is fucking Boston, not Vermont. People in this city want luxury, not recycled wood and energy efficient toilets that barely flush down the piss." I stepped back and shoved my hands into my pockets. He had no idea what he was talking about, and it became more obvious with each word he spoke. "I thought you would have learned from your daddy's mistakes." His eyes ran over the ceiling, traced the walls. "But it looks like the only thing you've inherited is his stupidity."

"Don't ever speak his name again."

"Or what?"

"Or I'll make sure it's the last thing you ever say."

His lip curled and his eyes narrowed. "You're shit. And this…this *Timber Towers*…is nothing but shit."

"Get the fuck out."

Had it been up to him, he probably would have casually turned around and strolled through the door. But it was no longer up to him. I nodded, and the two guards who stood at his sides took him by the arms and, as he swore and spat at them, they dragged his feet across the floor until he was outside.

"Do you think he knows something?" Will asked.

I watched them pull Randy down the sidewalk and put him into a cab. "Doubt it. He's nervous about the Hull deal, which he should be. He's getting fucked, and the fact that he doesn't know that makes him the stupid one."

"Then why would he come here?"

"I think he's starting to question his team and the people who are advising him, wondering if they're steering him in the wrong direction. He knows Timber Towers is better than anything he's ever gotten. He's got to be curious why that is."

"Tamra?"

I glanced at the door as the two guards walked back inside, and I thanked them as they made their way to the stairs. "I don't think he's on to her yet," I told him, "and she's not smart enough to play double agent."

"We need a new lead."

I nodded as I pulled out my phone. "You're right." And it had to be one who didn't want my dick.

He turned and headed back toward the office. "I'm going to grab my bag and lock up. I'll grab yours too."

"Thanks, buddy," I said, pulling up Hayden's last text.

Me: Find something on him. NOW. I want him fucking buried.
Hayden: What's got you so wound up?
Me: He came by Timber Towers.
Hayden: Oh shit. And?
Me: And he's lucky I didn't bury him under my foundation. I've had enough of his shit. We need something solid and we need it now.
Hayden: I know. I'm working on it.

I closed the text message window and saw the time on my home screen. *Fuck.* I was already late to meet Frankie. It would take me another few minutes to get to my Suburban and at least fifteen to drive there if I didn't hit any traffic or red lights. I pressed her number and listened to the four rings before her voicemail picked up. Then I hung up and immediately called her right back.

"Here," Will said, handing me my bag as I hung up. "Do

you need anything else?"

"I need Frankie to answer my goddamn call."

"Maybe she's not getting your call. The reception isn't great at The Hole."

"Or she's pissed that I'm late, and I didn't call to tell her."

"Want me to check the office lines to see if she left either of us a message?"

That would just waste more time. "I'm just going to take off." I shoved my phone into the front pocket of my flannel and headed toward the garage. "If you hear from her, tell her I'm on my way," I said over my shoulder.

"Got it."

I pulled out of the garage, relieved that the traffic wasn't thick through the Back Bay. I was able to take the side streets to avoid most of the lights and parked in a spot beside the restaurant. Frankie wasn't inside. I knew that even before I'd headed to our usual booth. I couldn't smell her, couldn't feel her eyes on me. My dick hadn't gone hard like it always did whenever she was near.

"She stayed about fifteen or so minutes and left, darlin'," the waitress said from behind me. It was Betty, the same server we'd had the last time we were here...the night I'd finger-fucked her underneath the table.

"She didn't happen to leave a message, did she?" A long shot, I knew, but I had to ask.

"I'd say the message on her face was loud and clear when she stormed out of here. She wasn't happy about the no-show, if you get my drift."

She hadn't seen my missed calls, or there hadn't been any because the service in here was shit. I'd let her down, and I was furious with myself for that. Now that she was pissed, I wondered if I should prepare myself for getting ignored... or worse.

"Thanks for the heads up, Betty."

"Do yourself a favor, darlin', and grab something nice and pretty for her. Girls like that. 'Course, they like wine, too. That might be your best bet, now that I think about it."

I laughed. "I'll keep that in mind."

TEN.

FRANKIE

I threw my purse down on the couch, kicked off my heels somewhere around the coffee table. One of the bottles Derek had sent was sitting in the wine rack unopened. It was staring at me, taunting me. If I didn't enjoy it so much, I would have thrown it out.

I poured myself a glass as I cursed him.

After twenty minutes of waiting with no phone call or text, I left the restaurant. He was the one who had asked for this dinner, the one who had set the time and place. The one who had confessed he wanted more from me, from us. And then, he didn't show up. The reason was irrelevant. Maybe he could pull that with the women he'd screwed before me, but I wouldn't tolerate it. I wasn't just some bimbo he picked up one night at a bar. If I was going to take the next step with him—however far that step was—then he needed to respect me. I'd been in a relationship where I came last, my feelings pushed aside, my dignity barely intact. I wasn't about to do that again.

I swallowed half my glass and refilled it.

What was happening to me? I'd gone a whole year without any drama, with many nights spent alone and a few horrible first dates, and I had been okay with that. Work was what was important, and Brea and Anna and my father. And just as I began to move to a deeper emotional place with the one person I shouldn't be doing that with, I got stood up.

This wasn't going to work.

I could hear my phone ringing from the living room. I ignored it. The three people who really mattered had their own ringtones, and what I heard wasn't any of theirs. So I let it go to voicemail. If it was Derek, he could leave twenty voicemails—one for each of the minutes I had waited. I wasn't answering.

I was carrying the glass into my bedroom when the line by my front door began to ring. It was the one used by security and doormen. Someone was here to see me, and I could only assume that someone was Derek. But he wasn't on my list, which meant they wouldn't send him up without calling. And if I didn't answer, he'd just wait and wait until he grew tired and left. Kind of like I'd done at The Hole.

There was no way I was answering that phone either.

I stripped off my jeans with my free hand and shuffled out of them until they were on the floor in the hallway. My panties dropped somewhere around the doorway of my bedroom. I set the glass on my nightstand, flung off my shirt and unclasped my bra. The shades were still open as I climbed under the covers. The soft glow from the adjacent buildings showed how empty my bed was.

I stretched my legs over the cool sheets. I loved how silky

they felt against my skin, and how the wine ran through my veins and heated the center of my chest. My fingers slowly crawled down my breasts, past my navel and halted.

I needed this.

No—I wanted this.

And I was the one who decided I'd have it. Not Derek Block.

I spread my legs a bit wider and pressed the back of my head into the pillow as the pads of my fingers found the center of my folds. It wasn't the motion I'd grown used to in the last several days, and the strength of Derek's hand wasn't present. I couldn't smell his skin surrounding me. But none of that mattered. It was exactly what I needed, the caress of something familiar, a speed and pressure that would ultimately bring me to the same place.

Something I controlled on my own.

I kept my eyes closed and concentrated on the sensation. My breathing turned labored; my nipples became hardened peaks. His face was there, behind my lids…those electric blue eyes, that torturous beard that ravaged me. As much as I tried to push it away, to block it or think of something else— someone else, or no one at all—he always returned. I could almost feel his fingers on me, controlling the circles I was making around my clit. I could almost hear his dirty mouth telling me how good I felt, how wet and tight and warm I was.

Ahhhhh…that's it. Right there.

All for me.

Not him.

A burst of pleasure rippled through my stomach. My free hand gripped the edge of my pillow and squeezed as the passion continued to build. It sucked every bit of breath out of my lungs. A moan released; a shudder exploded. And then an ease swept across my chest and settled into my muscles.

With my eyes closed, I reached for the glass of wine and drained whatever was left. Even when I was angry at him, he still had so much control over me. I may have taken it by breaking his masturbation rule—again—but it was his face that had sent the orgasm shooting through me. It was the thought of him that brought the tremble, and the build, and the release, and my fingers were just the tools. I hated it. And I hated that he'd stood me up, left me sitting alone in that damn restaurant, waiting for him like some desperate fool.

But even more than those, I hated that he didn't seem capable of keeping his word.

ELEVEN.

DEREK

I hit the button for Will's extension and waited for the intercom to connect. "Can you come in here for a minute? I need to send Frankie something." I hung up and waited for him to appear in my doorway.

"She still hasn't returned your calls?" he asked as he entered.

"Not a goddamn word from her." It was fucking noon. I'd sent her a text on my way to her building last night, left two messages when I got there and was rejected by the doorman because I wasn't on her list. But that goddamn piece of shit who had woken us up two mornings ago to smooth things over with her and bring her coffee—he was on her list...the same fucker who had cheated on her—with my sister. Brea had sent an email early this morning that said if I needed anything to reach out to her directly. Frankie had passed me off. I was her client and, the last time she had been upset, I'd made her promise not to ignore me professionally.

This time, I was the one who'd fucked up. Knowing that made it even worse.

"So you want to send her something?"

"Yeah, something that'll really make her smile."

Will smirked. "How about an apology?"

Funny guy. "She'll get one of those, too. Let's start with a gift to break the ice." Showing up late to the restaurant and not calling wasn't a good move, especially after telling her I wanted something more. I had to make it right. Then I'd come in with an apology...one she'd have no choice but to forgive.

"No lingerie or wine or flowers this time?" he asked.

"Nah, I've got to try something different."

"Give me a direction."

I remembered how much Frankie had loved her spa day at the hotel. "She likes being pampered." Her happiness didn't just come from getting her nails done. Whenever she spoke about Brea, her face took on a different glow. "Her relationship with Brea goes beyond work. They're best friends; they like to drink wine and..." I thought about the time I had run into them at the restaurant. "They're protective of each other. They make each other laugh." My eyes fell to my desk, remembering the clothes she had stripped out of. "She wears a lot of blue, and it looks damn good on her." I thought about the night we had stayed at the hotel, the way her eyes had lit up when she gazed out the window. "And she loves watching the sunset."

"Jesus."

"What?"

"What? I really need to elaborate?" He held his phone in his hand to take notes, but I didn't know that he had actually typed anything. "I'm not sure I heard a thing you just said. You lost me after 'pampered.'"

He was mocking me. "So I like her. What the fuck is wrong with that?"

"I don't know…what the fuck *is* wrong with that?"

His point was made.

"So what, then?" I asked.

"You keep talking about her and wine…there's a winery in Maine that's about three and a half hours from here. They give private tours and tastings, and there's a nice hotel not too far from there."

"Book it for her and Brea. A spa day, too, and hire a driver to take them there and back."

"I'll put something together and have it delivered to her in the next hour." He turned and left.

"Thanks, Will," I called out.

It was a good gift, not forcing her to spend time with me, but with her best friend. It would show her I wasn't just all about myself; that her feelings mattered too. And it was something I thought she'd really like…until I got her email a few hours later.

FROM: Jordan, Frankie
TO: Block, Derek
SENT: April 30, 3:29pm
SUBJECT: Your gift.

Thank you for the gift. However, I can't accept it. A messenger will be returning it. My forgiveness can't be bought, Derek, and I'm appalled that you would even try.

She was angrier than I thought. It made me want to lick those spicy lips and feel their fire. If she thought that email was going to deter me, she didn't know me at all. Without realizing it, she had given me what I'd wanted and that was a response.

FROM: Block, Derek
TO: Jordan, Frankie
SENT: April 30, 3:31pm
SUBJECT: YOUR gift.

If you don't want it, then give it to Brea. I'm not taking it back.
I'll be at your office at 7:00. We need to talk.

FROM: Jordan, Frankie
TO: Block, Derek
SENT: April 30, 3:32pm
SUBJECT: I just laughed out loud.

If you need to talk, call Brea's extension. She can help you with anything you need.
I won't be here at 7:00, and neither will you.

My hands clenched over my keyboard, a keyboard I wanted to rub over her pussy, teasing her with every key, so I could keep a taste of her in my office.

She knew I wanted her, that my dick was hard when I was around her and she was denying me. Testing me. She was making me work harder than I ever had.

My pink ivory was so fucking worth it.

FROM: Block, Derek
TO: Jordan, Frankie
SENT: April 30, 3:34pm
SUBJECT: 7:00 tonight.

I'll be at your building and I expect you to let me in. If not, you'll have to leave eventually and I'll be in the lobby when you do. I'll sleep there if I have to.

I watched the screen, waiting for her reply to come in. She had more power over me than I'd ever allowed a woman to have, and she was using it to control me. But she was hurt, and she had every right to be. I *would* fix it.

I would fix all of it.

FROM: Jordan, Frankie
TO: Block, Derek
SENT: April 30, 3:43pm
SUBJECT: Make it 6:00.

You'll get five minutes, before I head out for the night. Nothing more. And don't be late.

I wouldn't be late. And because I intended on making things right, I wouldn't be leaving without my tongue going inside her pussy. Whatever plans she had, she would be canceling. Tonight was our night together. She didn't know that yet...but she would soon.

TWELVE.

FRANKIE

I heard Derek's knock on my front door, but I halted before opening it. He needed to know I wasn't standing by, rushing to him just because he appeared. He needed to learn how to wait.

When I finally cracked the door, he was leaning against the frame, much closer than I expected. I smelled him instantly: spice, cedar, cold fall air. All man. His beard had been trimmed, but it was still bushy and full, though neater around the edges. His dark jeans outlined his muscular thighs; a red and white flannel hugged his chest. There was a time when I would have been turned off by his appearance, when I had considered it coarse and off-putting. Now I looked at him and my body filled with lust.

How could I be so furious with him, so disappointed, and still want him this much?

I could have easily wrapped my hands around his collar and pulled him against me, begging him with kisses to take me right there in the entryway. But that would have proven nothing but the power he had over me. There would be no consequences for his inconsideration.

I deserved an apology. And until that happened, nothing else would.

"Are you going to let me in?"

That voice…it was probably safer to shut the door and tell him we could discuss whatever he wanted, but it would have to be over the phone.

Knowing he would never agree to that, I turned and walked away, moving into the kitchen. I hadn't had a drink yet, and I hadn't had a desire to until I saw his face and now everything inside me was screaming for a splash of liquid calm. As I glanced over my shoulder, his eyes rose from my ass and slowly met mine. That made me smile, but I didn't let him see it. I'd worn these yoga pants and tiny tank top just for him because of how much of my body they showed. "Want a drink? I have beer."

"What kind?"

"An IPA." I'd kept some on hand after he'd spent the night, but I would never admit that to him.

"Perfect." He left a gap, during which I said nothing. "Thank you."

That was different.

I poured one into a mug and handed it to him, got a glass of wine for myself and made sure the granite island stayed between us at all times. He backed up against the fridge and stared into my eyes…and I let him. He was the one who finally broke the silence. "I shouldn't have left you waiting at the restaurant. It was wrong."

"You're right. It was."

He tilted his chin and gazed at me through his lashes. They

were long and thick, and the blue of his eyes looked even deeper in this light. I could feel his hands on my body, his lips on my nipples when he looked at me that way. It almost made me stop breathing.

"I'm sorry, Frankie."

"I know."

He smirked.

"Apology accepted."

He stepped forward toward the island and set his mug down, leaning into the counter. "That doesn't sound sincere."

I shrugged. "It's as sincere as it's going to get."

"Tell me what will make you happy."

As much heat as I was feeling on the inside, I remained cold when speaking to him. "I want an explanation…why you'd make plans with me and then stand me up."

"I'm not used to explaining my actions." He took a deep breath. "Hayden is the only person in my life who demands things from me. No one else dares to."

"Well, *I* dare to, Derek. Your dominance doesn't intimidate me."

The expression on his face was animalistic. "It should." He took a step closer. "Because do you know what I want to do to you right now? I want to slide you up against that wall," his eyes pointed to the one behind me, "clench your earlobe between my teeth, and tell you how good you feel, while I fuck your ass so hard, every soul in this goddamn building will hear your moaning…"

My God.

Moisture began to dampen my folds. I'd felt his fingers in that hole, but never his dick. I didn't know if I could handle it. The thought was as nerve-wracking as it was exciting.

I took a sip of my wine, holding it in my mouth while I contemplated which direction to take this. "I'll make a deal with you."

"There are no deals."

"I can very easily ignore the apology you just gave me and ask you to leave. So I suggest you hear me out."

He ran his fingers over his beard, a low growl coming from his lips. "What do you have in mind?"

"I'll give you my ass, but you have to explain to me what happened last night."

"When I want your ass, I'll take it."

"Appease me, or you won't be taking anything from me… ever."

He stared at his hands that were wrapped around the edge of the counter, his fingers turning white from his grip. "As I was leaving Timber Towers to meet you last night, someone stopped by unexpectedly. Getting them to leave took longer than I intended." I remembered that tone: it was the one he had used the night of the gala when we had been interrupted on the patio. "I called you before I left, but you didn't answer. When I got to the restaurant, you were already gone."

"Who was it?" If his tone hadn't changed so drastically, I wouldn't have asked, but the person was obviously significant. I wanted to know about the part of his life that he wouldn't let me into, even if it was just a peek.

"Someone I have a long history with. But don't worry, if I'm ever late again, you will get a phone call."

"Was it a woman?"

His teeth clenched. "No. It was a man."

"What's his name?"

"It doesn't matter. I took care of it."

It did matter. All of this mattered.

I moved to his side of the counter, stopping when there was just a foot of space between us. "What you've told me is probably more than you've told anyone in a while—maybe ever. But Derek, you were relentless the other night when you were trying to pull information out of me and—"

"His name is Randy. Now turn the fuck around and put your hands on the counter."

"The same man from the gala?" I asked, ignoring his command.

His hands moved to my waist, gripping it so tightly I could feel the anger pulsing through his body and the breath halting in mine. "Yes."

"Why do you hate him so much?"

His rough exhale blew into my face. I didn't know how it was possible, but the scent of it made me even wetter. "When you fuck with the people I care about, you become an enemy… and if you hurt them, I will destroy you."

A shiver ran through my body.

"Which category does he fall into?"

This was more than he had ever shared, more than I thought I would get out of him. If I had heard anyone else say this, I might have been frightened. But Derek's protective nature was comforting.

His gaze shifted between my eyes, his hands tightened on my waist. "I've held up my end of the deal."

The tone of his voice told me his answer, and it only led to more questions. Who was Randy? And why did Derek want to destroy him?

"You have," I agreed. He watched my hand as I touched his stomach. I could feel the hardness of his abs, even through the thick flannel. My fingers made a circuit around his defined chest, then I wrapped my arms around his neck. "Before I give you what you want, I need something from you."

His exhale was rough again. "Then ask."

I tilted my neck back and looked up at him, shifting my body even closer. His erection pressed into me, intensifying the throb between my legs as I held onto his neck even tighter. "I want you to kiss me."

THIRTEEN.

DEREK

Feeling her weaken in my hands as she asked me to kiss her was more fuel than I needed. I held her even tighter and lifted her. She squealed when she found herself in the air. I set her on the countertop, shoving the basket of fruit and stack of magazines out of my way.

"I was going to eat those," she said, staring at the bananas on the floor.

I gripped her cheeks, dragging her face toward mine. "I'll buy you more." And then I devoured her, giving her the kiss she had asked for. I wanted to make her cunt drip from just my lips pressing against hers and my tongue slowly gliding into her mouth. Her breathing told me how ready she was, so did her hands as they pulled at the buttons on my shirt. I stopped her. "Put your hands on the edge of the counter. The only time you move them is if I tell you to. Understood?"

"But what about—"

"No questions. Just enjoy this, Frankie."

As she smiled and followed my command, I removed her tank top. There was no bra beneath it; that had been evident since she'd answered the door. Her nipples were harder than the stone she sat on. They stared at me, taunting my teeth as I tugged her tight pants off, but left her red lace panties on.

I stepped back to take a look at her, with her legs spread over the granite and her hands gripping it submissively, and her hair tousled and falling over her tits. "Fuck, Frankie." What the hell had I done to deserve someone this beautiful, this stunning, who willingly gave me her body and let me do anything I wanted to it?

I was a lucky man. I had finally realized it.

Now, I was intent on appreciating it.

I walked to her wine rack, took the bottle she had poured from earlier, and brought it back to the island. I held it between her legs.

"What are you doing with that?"

"No questions." She was smiling; I wanted to lick that grin off her face. "Just kiss me, Frankie."

Her tits pressed against my neck the same way her mouth locked to mine. My cock rubbed on the inside of my jeans, pounding to be released and sunk into her warm snugness. Our tongues circled, and I teased mine deeper into her mouth, hinting at what I would do to her pussy.

When her kisses turned greedy, almost as demanding as her fingers had been, I pulled back. "Take those off." I motioned to her panties and watched as she wiggled them down. "Now lie back." She laid across the stone and I pulled her ass to the edge. She wrapped her legs around me and ran her feet over the backs of my thighs, over my ass and down again. "Keep gripping that counter and don't let go."

I poured some of the wine over her navel, and she moaned. The dark liquid pooled in her belly button. I leaned forward, placed my mouth over the hole, and sucked it dry. "That feels... so good," she said. I drizzled more over her, this time on her ribcage. It ran over the sides of her and onto the counter. I caught as much as I could in my mouth, licking my way along her ridges. Then I pointed the bottle between her tits and let it run over them, trailing down her stomach and washing over her pussy. My tongue followed, heading for her clit so I could lap it all up.

I could tell this was something she had never done before, she was having a hard time staying still. Her grunting filled the silence as my tongue flicked over her clit, licking from side to side, trying to catch every bit of wine while the sensations built inside her.

"Oh my God."

"Not yet," I demanded.

"But I..."

"Not yet!"

My nose pressed against the top of her pussy; my lips were buried inside, and my tongue plunged so fucking deep she was able to ride it. And she did...the wine dripped out of her navel and ran down her thighs, into her sweet, soft cunt. It tasted so goddamn good.

"I can't stop it," she cried. "I can't..."

I wanted to have her like this for hours, but I wanted to feel her come, too. "Then do it right now." My order sent quivers through her whole body, her pussy clenching around my tongue while waves of pleasure spread over her stomach.

"Oh *shiiiit*!" she screamed, until she stilled.

I stopped licking and slowly pulled my face out from between her legs. I wiped the moisture off my beard, but only because it was mixed with wine. Had it just been her juices, I would have left it, treasured it. Tasted it again and again until I showered in the morning.

She finally opened her eyes, loosened her grip on the counter, and looked down at me. "In the restaurant, you told me you were going to pour wine all over me, just like you told me you were going to use your flannel to tie me to your headboard. I guess I shouldn't doubt you when it comes to getting me off."

I washed my face at the sink, then dampened a paper towel and brought it over to her. She made me smile, and I didn't hide it. "No, you shouldn't." I wiped her pussy, cleaning her off gently.

"Sit up now."

I washed her tits, pausing to softly flick my tongue over each nipple. They grew as I sucked them into my mouth and brushed my teeth over the ends. "I can't get enough of you," I said, finally pulling my tongue away. Her gunmetal eyes stared into mine. She had forgiven me; she had even gotten me to open up a little. There was more I could do, more reassurance I could give. "I will never disrespect you that way again. You have my word, and as I've proven to you my word is my bond."

Her eyes softened, her fingers lifting to brush over my beard. "Thank you."

"Don't thank me yet." I dropped the paper towel and reached my hands around her, cupping her ass cheeks. "You gave me this tonight."

"I did."

"As much as I just want to take it, I won't unless you really give it to me. Is that what you're doing?" She chewed on her lip as though she were thinking about my question. Her cheeks turned flush, her hands continuing to brush over my whiskers. "Before you answer that, answer this: do you trust me?"

"Yes."

"Then trust me when I say I would never hurt your body."

A smirk crossed her mouth. "Never?"

"The pain won't be intended to hurt you, but to please you in a completely new way." I tugged her hands off my face and used my beard to skim around her nipple. "In a way you've never felt before." I moved back to her lips. "If I don't think you can handle it, I'll stop. If you don't think you can handle it,

I need you to tell me. But I need you to trust me, Frankie."

"I trust you," she whispered. "So, yes…I'm giving it to you."

FOURTEEN.

FRANKIE

I laid on my back in the center of the bed, watching Derek roll the condom over his dick and climb onto the mattress. My knees bent instinctively, my thighs rising until they pressed into my stomach. I felt him at the entrance of my ass.

"Trust me." His voice was as rough and raw as his beard, the bristles that were now brushing against my thighs as his tongue swiped down my…pussy—a word he made me want to use now. He dropped lower and lower, until his mouth finally reached my ass.

"Oh!" My back lifted off the bed in response. "I trust you," I breathed, reminding myself as much as him. I'd never felt a tongue on that spot, never felt soft wet pressure in that area. He was drenching my hole, probing it with the tip of his tongue. He was teasing my clit with his fingers at the same time. Having him down that low was such a foreign sensation. But tantalizing—naughty and taboo, even, which made it all the more erotic.

"There isn't a part of your body that doesn't taste delicious."

I couldn't keep from blushing as his words vibrated against my ass cheeks. He hadn't been there more than a few seconds, and already a sensation was building inside me. It was different from my usual orgasm; this was more concentrated on the lower part of my stomach, a warming that ended with small tingling bursts. He sensed the tension and slowed down, stopping the build as he moved back up my body. "Kiss me."

"Derek—"

"Fucking kiss me, Frankie."

I couldn't deny the face that stared back at me. He was gorgeous and demanding and controlling, and I wanted all of it…around me, on me, and most definitely inside me. As his mouth ravished mine, he gently inserted his finger—just a bit, like he had done the last time he'd been in this spot, allowing me to get used to it. As I began to move with him, he gradually increased his speed and pressure. One finger eventually turned to two, then three; he rubbed my clit at the same time. I found myself not just moving from the pressure, but actually grinding against it. Through my moans, I was begging for more.

And more is what he gave me.

His fingers were replaced by the tip of his dick. "Trust me," he repeated.

I closed my eyes, keeping my mouth on his, taking in his tongue at the same time I was taking in his cock. His mouth affected me tremendously, bringing out the most intense sensations. With the combined rubbing on my clit and the crown of his dick pushing into me, my body didn't know which one to focus on, which sensation was causing it to scream out in pleasure.

"If it hurts," he said, "you need to tell me to stop."

There was a slight burning feeling as he moved in deeper and my ass worked to take in more. It became much more pleasurable when my body fully accepted him. Even when it had, he didn't thrust inside me with all his power. He moved at a pace I could handle, one I was comfortable with.

"Derek," I moaned.

He growled, his lips traveling to my neck, just under my jaw where my pulse throbbed. "I knew you'd like it." He punched his hips forward until he was completely surrounded by me. "*Fuuuck*," he hissed. "I've never been inside anything this tight before."

I could feel what he meant, how my ass hugged him as he slid through all the slickness. Some of the lubricant had come from his licking; the rest I had created on my own. "Oh God," I grunted as he started moving faster. He was gliding out to his tip and shoving back in. His fingertips were swirling over my clit.

I gripped his shoulders, digging my nails into his skin. I didn't want to hurt him, but I needed to hold on so something other than this bed could bear some of the pleasure that was streaming through my body.

"Harder," he insisted.

"My nails?"

"Claw me fucking *harder*, Frankie."

I couldn't imagine that stabbing his skin felt as good as what he was doing to me, but his request combined with the sounds that came out of him was such a turn on.

"You're too tight," he said. "I'm…going to come."

I almost laughed. "That's a bad thing?"

"I need so much more of this before either of us even think about coming."

"More?" I shuddered. "But I'm almost ready now."

"Don't you dare!" He sat up taller on his knees,

straightening his body and pulling my legs so they straddled his waist. My back raised off the bed, my arms holding most of my weight. The new position gave him more freedom to go as deep or as shallow as he wanted. His hands returned—one on my clit, circling it with a fierce speed, and the other on my nipple. He tugged it and pinched it between his fingers.

So much building was happening inside my body. The way he rubbed my clit triggered a burst in my navel...the steady pumping in and out of my ass caused a desire that spread and peaked again and again in an endless wave. Even the clamping of my nipples caused a prickle to travel through my whole chest. The sight of his face was the only thing that kept me in the moment. Otherwise, the combination of it all would have overtaken me, and I'd have been shuddering on his dick in seconds. And I wouldn't do that...not until he gave me permission—partly because I enjoyed giving him that bit of power, and partly because the challenge of holding off my orgasm was as pleasurable as having one.

"Your fucking ass, Frankie...I'll never be able to get enough of it."

I covered his hand with mine as he pinched my nipple, and I squeezed his fingers so he gripped the small pebble even harder. He groaned when he realized what I was doing, complied and squeezed with the force I wanted.

My head drove into the mattress. "Derek...*ahhhhh*."

"Your ass is getting even wetter."

"It's you." I tilted my head forward so I could look at him again. "It's what you're doing to me."

He jerked forward, giving me quick, hard thrusts. I screamed after each one. "If I don't stop soon, my dick is going to break this condom and I'm going to fill your fucking ass with cum."

His dirty words always sent me so close to the edge. "Come, Derek...please," I begged.

"I want you to come before I do." My eyes closed, my feet tightened around him. "So you come first, Frankie. Come *right fucking now*."

I was already there; I had practically been there since the moment the burning had stopped. My muscles, my navel, my breasts—they all started to boil right before he pumped me to a screaming peak. I didn't know where the orgasm was born, which part of me felt the most pleasure or what was contracting, shaking, shuddering. But I felt it from inside me, outside me. I moaned through it until I ran out of breath. Then I watched him have his—his eyes pierced mine right before he ravaged my lips, his grunts spreading over my face, his hands gripping me in such a way that I could feel his pleasure as much as my own.

We finally stilled, and I felt him move next to me, gently brushing his fingertips over my nipples. They were more sensitive than they'd ever been.

"I had no idea something like *that* was even possible," I confessed, "especially from inside of *there*."

Derek propped himself up on his arm, running his fingers over my cheek and through my hair. "I told you I'd be your first for many things, and I promise you're going to like them all."

"If they feel anything like that, consider me your lifelong pupil."

His thumb pulled on my lip. I loved it when he did that, when he focused on my mouth and nowhere else. It made me feel like he was longing to kiss me, and kissing Derek Block was one of the most overpoweringly personal experiences I'd ever felt. He was rough and unrefined, robust and all man. His mouth had been all over my body, in places where no one had ever been before. But kissing was so intimate and soft—an emotional expression more than a sexual one. He didn't show a lot of emotion, but he did when his mouth was on mine.

"So submissive," he whispered.

"Only with you."

He cocked his head. "That means there are no others."

It wasn't a question; he was too demanding for that. He already knew the answer, but maybe there was a part of him that needed reassurance, the same way I had needed his earlier.

"No, Derek. There are no others. Just you."

"I like that answer even more."

FIFTEEN.

DEREK

I sat in my Suburban in the parking lot outside the motel. My eyes traveled up the stairs and across the doors until I saw 212. This was the room Tamra was in. She'd called a half hour ago and asked to see me immediately. I tried to push for a different date, another time; she wouldn't budge. Will was in a vendor meeting offsite and hadn't been able to plan an escape for me. Before leaving Timber Towers, I'd asked one of the assistants to call and make up an excuse that required me to get back to the jobsite. I hoped the time I had chosen would get me out of there before Tamra decided to take her clothes off...I needed to get my dick out of this mess, but I didn't know how. Tamra was our only contact, the only source we had who was inside Randy's circle. Without her, I would have no knowledge of his dealings, and I couldn't jeopardize that just yet.

I got out of the SUV, climbed the stairs and knocked on the door. I had a feeling she'd be wearing something sheer and tight and would do everything in her power to get me to touch her. I'd bailed the last two times I'd been in her presence; she wasn't going to let me get away with a third. And hell, I was right. She opened the door in nothing but light pink panties and a matching bra, her nipples so hard they made the fabric buckle.

I kept my eyes on hers. "Risky to be answering the door in just that."

"No one would be knocking on it besides you, baby."

My stomach churned. I wasn't her fucking baby. I wasn't her anything. She was lucky I was still standing there. I wasn't sure if this was even worth it anymore.

I stopped her when she reached for me, clamping her wrist for a second before pulling my hand away. "Don't make me remind you."

"Don't make me remind *you*, Derek." Her voice was whiny and pleading. "You haven't touched me in so long, I'm beginning to think you're using me."

I almost laughed, but it would have only confirmed that she was right. "Don't start. You know how this works."

"I do, and it seems like I'm the one doing all the giving and you're doing all the taking. It's my turn to take." She walked to the bed and took a seat on the edge of the mattress. She ran one of her heels up and down her leg as if she were sanding her skin. "Like them?"

The heels must have been the gift I'd had Will send her. "I picked them out for you, didn't I?" It was a pathetic lie…and a pathetic answer. But her smile told me it had satisfied her.

"You did, thank you."

"You didn't ask me here to talk about your shoes, and you know better than to call me just to service your pussy. If you have something to tell me, then say it."

She reached down and rubbed her clit over her panties. "Randy closed on the land in Hull a few days ago."

I looked at her feet. "Move your hand."

"But I want to—"

"Move your fucking hand. You don't touch yourself unless I tell you to."

She sighed. "Fine."

I waited, hoping for more. Nothing came. "That's it? That's all you have to tell me?" I was losing my patience and trying not to make it so obvious, but I couldn't stand seeing her in lingerie, or that I was even here, or that after all these goddamn years Hayden and I hadn't been able to secure a different source.

"Well, no," she said. "I've been looking at all the numbers and I ran a few more comps and I'm beginning to wonder if the land is actually worth what he paid. I mean, once the investors pulled out, I questioned it, but Randy knew I had a friend in banking and pushed hard for me to connect them."

"Good deal or not, it shouldn't affect you."

"But it does."

It all clicked into place then. If any part of me had wondered whether Tamra had ratted me out to Randy, I had just been reassured that she hadn't.

"You're not getting your commission, are you?"

She shook her head. "Turns out, it's all happening off the books. I brokered the damn deal and I'm not getting shit! Can you believe that cheap fucking bastard wasn't going to tell me? Probably planned to drag it out for as long as he could, then lie about the funds or something…like I haven't been sucking the lenders dick and getting all the inside scoop." Her eyes widened. "Sorry. I probably could have left that part out."

I wasn't focused on whose dick she was sucking; I was focused on the transferring of the money. Tamra's commission must have been kicked back to the lender, which was how Randy would pay the extra points. He couldn't afford to pay it any other way. Had he come to Timber Towers to gloat over his win, or to drool over mine? "So the deal is absolutely done?"

"The money was already wired and not one dime of it is coming to me. He even had the balls to ask me to look for more properties. He wants Boston, Back Bay—as close to your building as I can find."

"What have you shown him?"

It looked like all the air had been sucked out of her body, wilted on that bed like a discarded balloon. "I haven't looked. I needed a few days to cool off." Her hand dropped to her thigh. "So now do you see why I'm not in such a giving mood?"

Randy had financially fucked her. I felt bad about that. Although she had never been loyal to him, she had worked as hard as she was capable of, and that had to count for something. "I get it," I said.

"Will you get my mind off it, Derek? Come over here and make me feel better…"

I crossed my feet and leaned into the dresser. "Are you quitting your job?"

"I want to. He's been acting so crazy lately, scrambling to buy anything he can get his hands on." Her fingers paused at the edge of her panties. "I want you to hire me, Derek. I'll give you a little head over lunch…my ass over dinner. We'd make such a good team." She sounded excited about the arrangement.

My phone dinged from the front pocket of my flannel. I pulled it out and read the text from Hayden:

I got what we need, brother. He's finished. FINISHED. Be at my place at 7:00 tonight.

Hayden practiced fact, not theory. She wouldn't have sent it unless she was positive this new source was a strong one. It wasn't time to celebrate; it was time to get the fuck out of this motel room. The disaster who was spread eagle across from me with her fingers on the verge of plunging into her cunt was no longer needed.

But I couldn't cut her off completely. Tamra had been a good source. Needy, whiny, demanding to the point where her punishments got rougher than I'd intended…but she'd been loyal. That was something I couldn't forget.

"What if I got you a job? Not with me, but with someone I think you'd work really well with." Someone who liked to use her mouth as much as Tamra did. I wasn't positive I could make it happen, but Will had been dropped off at work this morning, and the woman in the backseat looked suspiciously like Julia.

She started to stand. "You'd do that for me?"

"I would." I put my hand in the air to stop her from coming any closer. "But what's going on between us has to end."

"It was the dick-sucking comment, wasn't it?" It was too stupid a question to even consider answering. "I knew it as soon as I said it."

"I'm going to head out and let you get dressed. I'll be in touch once I hear something. In the meantime, stay with Randy. I'll get you out of that job soon enough." I gave her a nod and moved toward the door.

"Hey, Derek?"

I looked over my shoulder.

"Thank you." She sounded sincere.

"You got it."

I got back inside my Suburban and pressed the number for Frankie's cell.

"Calling me during the day…this must be serious," she said. Her voice was like a scalding shower, washing away every image of Tamra that lingered in my head.

"Bad news, baby."

"You're canceling our plans tonight."

I hated how disappointed she sounded. I never wanted to be the reason she was upset, or be the cause of her anger or sadness. I only wanted to make her smile…and moan. It was a disconcerting realization—one I wouldn't let myself really think about.

"I have no choice." I turned at the light, heading back toward the city. "Something big has come up."

"With work?"

She wanted more from me, and I knew that, in the same way I wanted more from her. When it came to Randy, I'd already broken the seal with her. It wouldn't hurt to give her a bit more. "It's not exactly work-related." I pounded my fingers on the steering wheel. Talking about it was harder than I thought. "It's Randy. Hayden uncovered something, and she wants to discuss it."

"Are you free right now?"

I glanced at the time on my dashboard. Will would be in that vendor meeting for at least another hour; the crews would call if something came up. "I have some time…why?"

"Come to my office." She didn't sound hurt anymore. Her tone was similar to when my tongue was on her.

My balls began to ache, my dick pushing against my fly. Just the thought of being with her in that office made me so goddamn hard. "Should I bring anything?"

"Just you."

SIXTEEN.

FRANKIE

"Mr. Block is here," Brea said after I picked up the phone.

"Please send him in." I ran my fingers under my eyes to catch any loose powder that had fallen and fluffed the sides of my hair. "And remember, no staff interruptions until I give you the okay."

"I've got it handled, don't worry." I hadn't told her my plan, but she knew—she knew *everything*...like how keeping Derek interested took work and how I was trying things I'd never done before. I planned to do both today.

I felt him before my eyes found him in the doorway. His stare was fierce and captivating; it hit my breasts, the folds between my legs. It stirred a chaos of emotions.

"Frankie…"

"Lock the door." I realized I had given him an order and added, "Please."

He turned the knob and tucked his hands into his pockets.

I had wondered how it would feel to have Derek in my office, a space much more formal and colder than my condo. My father liked to keep things ultra-contemporary with sharp lines and random blasts of color. He believed this style screamed wealth, which was what we needed to portray to our book of business and potential clients.

Derek's casual, almost lumberjack style didn't seem to clash with the décor. What really screamed in here was my need for him, my desire to be closer and to feel his power in my hands. "Come here," I said.

His stance widened, and he glanced at his boots. "I don't know what you have planned, but I'm the one who does the demanding." His eyes locked with mine. "Not you."

I walked to him and grabbed his hand, holding it in front of my pussy so he could feel the heat coming off me. "I'm not trying to control you, Derek." My free hand touched the outside of his jeans, running up and down his fly. "I'm just trying to show you what I want." It amazed me how much power his fingers could hold. How the grazing of one fingertip could make my wetness pool, how his hesitation to my command could make me desperate to try harder.

"What is it that you want?"

I led him to my desk and sat him in my chair. "Can I show you?" I waited for his nod, then I kneeled on the floor, tugging at the button and zipper of his jeans. I pulled his dick through the hole of his boxer briefs.

"Jesus, Frankie."

"No?"

His fingers wove into my hair as his palm held the base of my neck. "Yes. Hell-fucking- yes."

He was already fully erect…my mouth watered as I looked at it. The open windows allowed me to take in every detail, every beautiful inch, every pulsing vein. The bead of pre-cum gleamed on the tip. I licked it off and swallowed it.

"That fucking mouth," he hissed as I licked over his wide ridge. He held my head to maintain control, even as I worked him deeper between my teeth. "Shit, Frankie."

I covered the top of his shaft and swiveled around to the backside. My hand cupped his balls as I gently rubbed them around in my fingers. The last time I had given him a blowjob, he'd tied my hands so I couldn't pump him and suck him at the same time. I did it now, holding the base of his shaft while wrapping my lips around his crown.

"Milk it, baby."

I dipped my lips farther down, taking as much of him in as I could without gagging. As my mouth lowered, my fingers twirled around the base of him, my knuckles then sliding upward to meet my mouth. My spit dribbled down my palm, matching the slickness of my tongue.

Derek's grip tightened, fisting a handful of my hair, directing me up and down his dick. "Fucking milk it," he grunted. I let him feel as though he were leading me, but I wanted this probably more than him and to know I had the power to make him feel good. And when his cock banged against the back of my throat, I wanted him even more—more of his flavor, more of his skin, more of his cum.

I wanted to swallow his orgasm.

"You keep this up, and I'm going to come."

"Mmm…" I grumbled.

My hand pumped harder and faster, and when my mouth reached his tip, I sucked as deeply as I could. His hips moved with me, moaning with every stroke, every suck. "I'm warning you now; if you don't want my load in your mouth, then you'd better stop."

I just kept on sucking, my hand sliding all the way to his base, his shaft getting slicker as more of my saliva fell over him. When he stopped moving with me, I felt a change in his dick.

"Oh, fuck...*oh fuck*..." He was there, so I kept my lips around the tip and sucked even harder. "Take it, baby." Then he squirted into my mouth, a long, hot stream that coated my tongue and splashed against the back of my throat. "Take it all." A second stream shot in, then a third. The sounds he made were the same ones as when he was inside my ass, gripping my face with the same intensity as I had dug my fingernails into his shoulders.

I pulled back and sucked the cum off my tongue, swishing it around a bit before swallowing it down. As I did, my eyes never left his hard, passionate gaze. While the warm fluid ran down my throat, I tucked him back inside his boxer briefs and zipped him up.

He said nothing.

I stood only halfway before he grabbed me and pulled me onto his lap, wrapping his arms around my waist and covering my lips with his. "You're amazing...that fucking mouth is amazing."

I smiled, took his hand and led him to the door. Our experience in my office mirrored the one we'd had in his, when he'd summoned me and licked me on top of his desk. It seemed that I was returning the favor.

"Things with Hayden shouldn't take all night." He sounded calm, relaxed. No commands, no insistence. I liked this side of him.

"So what are you saying?"

"I'm saying...I'd like to come to your place when we're done."

Neither of us knew what time that would be, and I didn't want to miss the call from downstairs in case I was sleeping. "I'll put your name on the list. They'll let you right up." It was a big step, one I wasn't sure I was entirely ready for. But it was the next logical step. "I may be sleeping."

His lips pressed on the edge of my ear. "I hope you are so I can wake you with my tongue..." I moaned, the dampness between my legs growing. "And you'll be getting hours of it as a reward for how good you've been to me today."

I leaned back and met his eyes. There was a pang of need that made me want to leave this office and take him home right now. But the wait would make it all the more enticing.

"I'll see you later," he said, kissing me one last time.

I watched him walk out the door and say good-bye to Brea before he disappeared down the hall. Brea watched him too, then looked at me. "Good fucking God."

"I know."

"I was talking about you, too."

I winked. "I know."

She leaned on her desk. "Before we talk about what just happened…your dad called while you and Mr. Block were locked inside your sex cave. He wants to see you—right now. I made up an excuse to buy you a few minutes, but I suggest you get your hot ass down there."

"Oh, shit." I ran inside my office and took out my mirror, checking my hair and makeup. I flattened the strands Derek had frizzed, cleaned up my smudged eyeliner, applied more gloss so I'd look a bit more presentable and walked to his office. My father would be the first person to call me out if I wasn't completely put together. He liked perfection—he believed in nothing but.

"Come in, Frankie," he said. His door was already open and I stepped inside. "Take a seat."

I felt exposed, like he knew I'd been less than professional only minutes before. I tugged the bottom of my skirt to lengthen it as I sat and crossed my legs. We normally had our business chats first thing in the morning, at least an hour before any employees arrived. It was rare that he called me into his office mid-day. There had to be a problem with one of the agents. I was surprised I hadn't heard about it…

"Let's get right to it," he said, leaning back in his chair and resting his foot over the other thigh. His hands made a steeple under his chin. "The doctor has given me no choice but to step back a little. Because I need to spend less time here and less time focused on work, someone needs to take on more responsibility. I've designated that person to be…you." His chair swung back and forth. "I've given great consideration to which division I intend to hand over to you, and I've come to a conclusion…" He paused as though this were a game show, as though it had taken only a few right questions to get *here*.

But getting here had taken me more than half my life.

Jordan International was divided into three divisions: residential, commercial and leasing. My sales were solely focused on residential, but I was involved in all sectors as was my father. For him to choose a division meant I wasn't good enough to oversee all three…

I tried to focus on the moment as much as possible.

He picked up the silver pen lying on his desk and tapped it against a stack of papers. I held my breath as his mouth opened. "I'm giving you the residential division."

If I had to choose one, it would have been that; the most demanding of the three, the one I'd been prepping for since I had graduated college. I wanted to scream, but it wasn't appropriate—not in this office, and certainly not in front of my father.

"You've done well, Frankie. Extremely well, in fact. You've put all your attention on Jordan International, looked out for the company's best interest. You've put your job before yourself for nearly your entire adult life, which is exactly what I would expect from a CEO." Compliments from my father were rare, so I listened intently, taking it all in, relishing in this dream that was finally coming true. "I've never seen anyone sacrifice quite like you, especially since you broke things off with Reed. Landing Block Development was a significant highlight of your career. I wasn't sure you were going to pull it off; I'm incredibly impressed that you did."

Block Development.

Derek.

I clamped my fingers tightly under the edge of my chair, a stab of guilt gnawing at me.

"I heard Derek was in the building today…signing off on the two offers, I assume?"

I ran my tongue across my teeth. I could still taste him in my mouth.

Instead of presenting the offers to Derek, having him sign off or counter, I had sucked his dick. Was that something a dedicated employee would have done? How much had I really sacrificed if I was giving my biggest contract a blowjob in my office?

Who had I become?

Only one thought occurred: Julia.

I'd become *her.*

"No, he hasn't signed off on the contracts," I said.

"I trust you have everything under control." I just nodded. "I was hoping you'd bring him by so I could finally meet him. I expect you'll make that happen soon."

"I will."

"Good." He pushed the stack of papers toward me. "The transition is going to take place in stages. If you continue to prove yourself and grow the residential division, in six months I'll hand over the leasing division, and six months after that, the commercial division. I had the attorney draft up an agreement to make it official, to keep it all documented and the terms outlined."

The words on the first page were blurred from the tears I was holding back, but they weren't from happiness…they were from the disappointment that was eating its way through me. I wouldn't shed them in here.

I gathered the papers into my arms and stood. "I'll review them and return them once they're signed. Thank you. I'm honored, Dad. Truly honored." It was all I could say at the moment.

He smiled. "You'll make me proud—or prouder, I should say."

I didn't know how that was possible now.

I hurried to the door, but he called out before I could leave. "And Frankie? I may have given you the residential division because you worked extremely hard for it…but that doesn't mean you should take it for granted. I can rescind the offer as easily as I've extended it. I expect the new responsibilities will inspire you to work even harder now and to sacrifice even more of your personal time. Am I clear?"

"Yes. Very."

I couldn't think under his stare, under the pressure of the guilt that boiled in my chest. I would brush my teeth, pour myself a glass of wine and, once I had a clear head, I would look at the terms…this legal agreement he felt he needed with his daughter.

"Take a few days to review it all," he said. "We can talk about it when you're ready, my girl." His voice had suddenly lightened, a tone he didn't frequently use in the office.

I smiled at him, then turned around again and headed straight for Brea's desk. I grabbed her hand and dragged her into my office, shutting the door behind us.

"What happened?" she asked, taking a seat on the other side of my desk.

"Hang on a minute," I told her as I pressed Anna's number in my contacts.

"Hello?"

"Anna, it's me and Brea. I have you on speaker phone."

"Is everything all right, doll?"

"I wanted to tell you both this at the same time." Brea's brows raised; Anna stayed silent. "It happened."

"What happened?" Anna asked. Brea's eyes opened wide, and I knew she was thinking of something else entirely… something that included Derek.

Not that, I mouthed.

"My father gave me the residential division."

"Oh my God!" Brea squealed.

"Honey, that's wonderful news," Anna said. "I knew he would finally come around and give you what you deserve. Congrats, baby girl. I couldn't be prouder of you."

I stared at the stack of papers he'd given me and thought about what had happened in this office not fifteen minutes earlier. I'd kneeled, I'd sucked; I'd swallowed…my client. I couldn't believe it.

Things had changed since Derek had come into my life.

I had changed.

I shuffled through my appointments; I forgot to submit contracts. Aside from Block Development, I hadn't secured any new clients—all because my mind was elsewhere. I wasn't the woman my father had described, the one who sacrificed her personal life and stayed fully committed to the best interest of the company. The only thing I had been fully committed to was Derek's dick.

I was a mess.

And I was in total fucking lust with Derek Block.

"Yes," I said, "it's very exciting." The implications sank in. "It'll put me in charge of a massive team of people, people who depend on my leadership and mentorship, who count on me for their jobs." The guilt was rising into my throat, my eyes burning from still holding back tears. "He made it very clear that what I've sacrificed is nothing compared to what I'll have to sacrifice when I take over. If these last few weeks have proved anything, it's that I can't have what I want personally and professionally at the same time."

"Doll," Anna said kindly. "Please don't say what I think you're going to say…"

I kept my eyes off Brea as Anna's voice trailed off. I had told Anna very little about Derek the last time I was at her apartment, but it was enough for her to know I had feelings for him. "You two are the most important people in my life, and that's why I need your support on this decision. I can't keep moving in the same direction and still maintain control personally and professionally. It just isn't possible."

"Seriously?" Brea said.

"Yes. Seriously. I have to make a choice…" Brea shook her head and reached for my hand. I knew what she was going to say, what she wanted me to do. But this wasn't up to her, and it wasn't up to Anna. This was on me, and I had to do what was right. I had to do what was best for me. For my future.

"Whatever it is, doll," Anna said, "you have my support."

Brea nodded sharply. "Mine, too. Always."

I turned away from her and took a deep breath. "Then I choose…"

SEVENTEEN.

DEREK

Hayden poured two fingers of vodka into a short tumbler and slid it across the counter toward me. Then she poured the same in a second glass and kept it for herself, holding it up in the air. "A toast," she said, "to finally catching that bastard."

I clinked my glass against hers and downed the booze. "Are you going to tell me how we're going to do that, or are you going to keep me in suspense all night?"

She stared at my empty glass and placed hers next to it.

"You've heard the term 'ambulance chaser', haven't you?" I wasn't stupid. I nodded. "Our firm doesn't employ one because we don't need to and it's a practice we don't believe in. I've met several over the years, none who I thought I could really trust or do the job we need, but I met one recently who I thought could handle it. I hired him and hadn't heard a word from him until yesterday morning."

"You hired him through the firm?"

"No. I did it privately." She picked up her glass again and drained the drop that was left. "I guess the timing must have been right...because we got lucky."

Fucking Tamra was something I could live with; I had done it for my family and I would do it all over again. I didn't want any of that burden on Hayden; I wanted her hands to stay clean. Her involvement could have gotten her disbarred. It didn't sound like she had done anything illegal, but the look on her face and the tone of her voice told me she wasn't happy.

"What did he find?" I asked.

"There's a construction worker who was hurt at Randy's jobsite not too long ago. He's a long-time employee...still is."

It made sense now why Hayden didn't sound happy. If he was still employed by Randy, it must have taken some persuading to get him to swing. I was sure that involved cash. Hayden's hands were dirty now.

"There are more workers, Derek—many more...names that he'll eventually give me."

I ran my fingers over my beard as I processed it all. "He paid their medical bills, didn't he?" This was so fucking layered. "He gives them money to keep quiet."

"I think so."

"They're bleeding him dry; that's why he's out of cash." I remembered some of what Tamra had said in the motel room: Randy had been acting crazy lately, scrambling to buy anything he could get his hands on. He'd used her commission to pay points to his lender. He was stretched so thin financially; it was difficult to believe he was still in business. But I knew what helped him stay afloat: the shoddy construction, the cheap materials, the quick turnaround for permits and inspection.

"I'm going to bury him, Derek."

"Has he hired your firm?"

"We're working out those details right now."

There were many details, I was sure of that—some Hayden would eventually share with me, others that she was legally bound not to divulge. I wanted to hear it all. The man had ruined my family…every detail mattered.

"Does he know your affiliation?"

"No."

"Jesus, Hayden." I poured myself another shot of vodka and slammed it back. "Do you think he'll change his mind when he finds out?"

"One thing has nothing to do with the other."

I set the glass down and tried to calm the pounding in my chest. She was the attorney, the one who knew the law, but it didn't take a moron to know this case—and our affiliation—wasn't typical. "Are you sure about that?"

She sighed. "Let me get him signed with the firm and get his statement documented. If it comes up then, I'll deal with it. But I honestly don't know why it matters. He wants restitution for his pain and suffering and so do I. We're after the same thing, brother. I won't be leading the case—I can't, legally—but I'll be watching from the background with a hand heavily involved." I poured her another shot. "This is only the beginning. We're going to pull inspection records; we'll find offshore accounts if he has them, every person he has ever given money to or taken money from. It's going to be an extremely long and painful process for him. His entire world is about to explode."

My phone vibrated from my back pocket. On the screen was an email from Will, telling me he had spoken to Julia and she was happy to hire Tamra for her real estate team. I wanted to hear more about that conversation, but it would have to come later. I clicked off the screen and set my phone on the counter.

"You know once this all starts, you're going to be

questioned and you'll have to testify," she said. "You're going to have to give a detailed account of that entire day."

"I know."

"And because you have all the industry contacts, you're going to have to put me in touch with them." She moved to my side of the counter. "This is going to take a lot of time, Derek. I have to know you're as invested in this as I am."

"Don't question it. You know I am."

We'd promised each other we'd stay focused until we found a way to take Randy down…that had included not getting involved in a relationship—something I hadn't even considered until Frankie. Before she confirmed my single status, I needed to change the conversation. Better yet, I needed a break. "Bathroom," I said, "I'll be right back."

I walked to the powder room on the other side of the kitchen and shut the door behind me, gripping the edge of the sink. I'd get her whatever connection she needed; I'd help her research. I'd give a statement and tell the attorneys what I heard that day on the jobsite…what I saw. I'd testify in court. I'd play nice and let the legal system punish Randy for what he had done. But goddammit, I didn't want to give up Frankie. Not for my sister, not for anyone. But that was what it would take, and I knew she would ask it of me.

I stared at my reflection, trying to make sense of it all. I looked tired, haggard. My beard needed trimming, and I needed some sleep. Frankie's pussy would be keeping me up again all night. My dick twitched at the thought of that, at what she would look like when I walked into her room, the sheets lying over her delicious body. How she would taste when I slowly ran my tongue over her clit, rewarding her for the head she had given me today.

That fucking mouth.

There was no way I could give that up.

When I came out of the bathroom, Hayden was staring at the phone in her hand. She quickly tucked it behind her back when she saw me. "I wasn't completely honest with you the other day, Derek." I eyed her glass; she had poured more vodka since I'd been gone. "Frankie Jordan and I have a bit of a past."

"Don't go there, Hayden." I didn't know where this had come from, but I didn't like it.

"No—you're going to hear this." She paused. I knew she was reading my expression, testing my level of anger. This was difficult for her, and I wanted to make it easier, but I didn't think I could. "Reed Reynolds was a stranger, who I knew nothing about, when I met him at the bar. We went back to his place—a condo, I later learned, he no longer lived in because he had moved in with Frankie and was just too lazy to sell it. We were in his bed when she came in. She was out of breath, upset, tousled." Her voice started to soften. "His bed is on a platform several feet higher than the rest of the room, a set of stairs surrounds it." She sipped from the glass. "She grabbed his arm and, when he reacted, he pushed her. I don't think he meant to. It happened so fast...and it was dark." I felt something coming. Something I didn't want to hear. Something that would hurt me worse than it was hurting her. "She fell down the stairs, Derek...she screamed. When Reed turned on the light, Frankie didn't move. She just laid there on the hard floor, gripping her stomach like she was in pain, but nothing came out of her lips. No words, just tears...so many tears. I don't know how long she stayed like that, ignoring us, completely frozen, but it felt like an eternity. And when she finally sat up, there was blood—so much of it, running down her legs...and I knew." Oh fuck, no. "When I tried to help her to her feet, she wouldn't let me. I offered to take her to the hospital and she said no. She wouldn't accept Reed's help either. She just wanted to leave his condo. And we let her."

I wanted to reach for the vodka, but I didn't. I wanted to smash every piece of furniture in her kitchen, but I didn't do that either. I tried swallowing the knot in the back of my throat and breathed. "Say it, Hayden."

"She miscarried their child on his bedroom floor. Because of Reed. Because of me."

"Why are you telling me this?"

"Because you told me she's just your realtor and I believed

you. But why would your realtor send you this?" Her hand was now in front of my face, holding a phone that I quickly realized was mine. I'd gone to the bathroom so fast, I had forgotten it on the counter. The screen showed a text from Frankie:

I know you were planning on coming over tonight, but something has come up and I have to cancel. I won't have my phone on me, so if you call or text back, I won't get it. I'll explain everything to you in the morning. xoxo

I took the phone from her hand and slipped it into my pocket. "I'm not talking about this with you."

"Tell me something…do you receive hugs and kisses from every woman you do business with?"

"Hayden—"

"Because it looks to me like something is happening between you two. I felt it when I saw her at your townhouse, and I feel it now."

Goddammit, I didn't want Hayden to find out this way. Now that she knew, I didn't know how to fix it. And there was certainly no fixing her history with Frankie. The truth about that night at Reed's condo was much worse than I thought. All of it was…including the way my sister was looking at me right now.

Frankie's text was bothering me, too. Hugs and kisses? That didn't sound like her at all…if anything, it sounded like Brea. But why would Brea have Frankie's phone…and why would she be sending me texts on Frankie's behalf?

All of this was a fucking mess. I needed to get to the bottom of things. But first I needed to find Frankie.

"Listen, Hayden—"

"*Now* you want me to listen to you, brother? *Now* you suddenly have something you want to tell me? Why, Derek?" She threw her glass on the floor, shattering it. "*Why?*"

My phone vibrated, and I reached for it in my pocket. I needed a chance to breathe, to think of what I was going to say to Hayden, and reading the text message would give me that. But when I saw the first line, I knew I wouldn't be getting the break I wanted. From where Hayden was standing, she was able to see the screen and, from the sound of her gasp, she was reading it, too:

Frankie will always be mine. So will her womb. She's just waiting for me to put another baby inside it. Mine...not yours, asshole. You can keep that whore of a sister who's the worst fuck I've ever had. She's nothing but a cunt, anyway. Game on, motherfucker. —Reed

When Reed had come to Frankie's condo and I had mentioned Hayden to him, I didn't say she was my sister. Frankie hadn't either. That meant he had researched me...and he had probably figured out that my last name was different than hers.

Goddammit.

I slowly looked up, watching the emotion fill Hayden's face. "Oh my God, Derek..." I wished she hadn't seen that text. She was a strong one, but this situation was rough on her...and on Frankie.

Game on?

I gritted my teeth together. "I'm going to fucking kill him."

No, it was game over.

To be continued...

DID YOU ENJOY UNBLOCKED EPISODE THREE?

Reviews mean the world to authors, and they are the most powerful way to help other readers learn about my work. If you enjoyed *Unblocked Episode Three*, I would absolutely love it if you left an honest review. Even if it's short, as little as a few sentences, it can still help so much.

Also, don't forget to grab Episode Four, which is available now!

MARNI'S MIDNIGHTERS

Getting to know my readers is one of my favorite parts about being an author. In Marni's Midnighters, my private Facebook group, we chat about steamy books, sexy taboo toys, and sensual book boyfriends. Team members also qualify for exclusive giveaways and are the first to receive sneak peeks of the projects I'm currently working on. To join Marni's Midnighters, search for us on FaceBook.

ABOUT THE AUTHOR

Bestselling author Marni Mann knew she was going to be a writer since middle school. While other girls her age were daydreaming about teenage pop stars, Marni was fantasizing about penning her first novel. She crafts sexy, titillating stories that weave together her love of darkness, mystery, passion, and human emotions. A New Englander at heart, she now lives in Sarasota, Florida, with her husband and their two dogs, who have been characters in her books. When she's not nose deep in her laptop, working on her next novel, she's scouring for chocolate, sipping wine, traveling, or devouring fabulous books.

Want to get in touch? Visit Marni at www.MarniSMann.com or email her at MarniMannBooks@gmail.com

ALSO BY MARNI MANN

A Sexy Standalone (Erotica)

Wild Aces
Trapper Montgomery has been passed from one abusive home to another. They were all the same—the taste of blood on his tongue, the sound of broken bones in his ears. But when he finally escaped the system that tore him apart, he dedicated his life to avenging those who had laid their hands on him, who spit at him, who told him he was nothing. He was ready to fight…until he met Brea Bradley.

The Unblocked Collection (Erotica)

Episodes 1–5
Derek Block seeks revenge. Frankie Jordan seeks professional dominance. He wants her; she wants him. Lines that can't cross begin to blur. Things start heating up as real estate gets real…

The Shadows Series (Erotica)

Seductive Shadows
Charlie is a passionate, sensually inspired art student, desperately seeking an escape from the abusive past

that haunts her and a tragic accident that emptied her heart. Scarred and unable to love, her yearning for physical pleasure leads her into a tantalizing, dangerous world of power and seduction.

Seductive Secrecy
Can Charlie and Cameron overcome the destruction of their clouded pasts, or will the revelation of more painful, shocking secrets pull them back into the shadows?

The Bar Harbor Series (New Adult)

Pulled Beneath
Drew travels north to settle her grandparents' estate, but she finds more questions than answers as the truth starts unraveling. What she didn't expect to find was Saint, whose reputation is as tumultuous as his past. With Saint's scars so deep and Drew's so fresh, can the pair heal from their painful wounds, or will they be pulled beneath the darkness of their pasts?

Pulled Within
Rae Ryan has lived in a storm over which she has no control. Plagued by nightmares and a terrible family secret, she carries her scars as much on the inside as she does on the outside. Can she survive the storm and become a part of the light she so desperately desires? Or is she destined to remain pulled within?

The Memoir Series (Dark Fiction)

Memoirs Aren't Fairytales
Leaving behind a nightmarish college experience, Nicole and her friend, Eric, escape their home of Bangor, Maine, to start a new life in Boston, Massachusetts. Fragile and scared, Nicole desperately seeks a new beginning to help erase her past. But there

is something besides freedom waiting for her in the shadows—a drug that will make every day a nightmare.

Scars from a Memoir
Two men love Nicole; one fills a void, and the other gives her hope of a future. Will love find a way to help her sing a lullaby to addiction, or will her scars be her final good-bye?

#8.99

Made in the USA
Middletown, DE
31 January 2023